Secret Santa

Secret Santa

A NOVEL

ROBERT TATE MILLER
and
BETH POLSON

ATRIA BOOKS

NEW YORK   LONDON   TORONTO   SYDNEY   SINGAPORE

ATRIA BOOKS

1230 Avenue of the Americas
New York, NY 10020

Library of Congress Cataloging-in-Publication data is available.

ISBN: 0-7434-8797-4

First Atria Books hardcover edition November 2003

10   9   8   7   6   5   4   3   2   1

ATRIA BOOKS
is a trademark of Simon & Schuster, Inc.

Manufactured in the United States of America

For information regarding special discounts for bulk purchases,
please contact Simon & Schuster Special Sales at
1-800-456-6798 or business@simonandschuster.com

Secret Santa

CHAPTER 1

Rebecca Chandler's Christmas motto was simple: "Wake me when it's over."

It wasn't that she was a Scrooge, quite the contrary. Rebecca could bake reindeer-shaped cookies and wrap presents with the best of them. In the spirit of the holiday, she had served up turkey and stuffing at the local homeless shelter, and had even knocked out a few of those self-serving Christmas missives, chronicling the humdrum lowlights of yet another year in her boring life.

Rebecca forced herself through the merry motions,

but, in reality, she found the demands of the season as appealing as a year-old fruitcake. There were three things in life she detested merely as a matter of principle: shopping, waiting in line, and holiday music. December invariably brought all three.

Rebecca avoided the holidays by doing what any self-respecting, young newspaper reporter would do, by working 24–7.

"Chandler!" the editor's voice thundered across the newsroom. Rebecca didn't even flinch. She had long since grown used to Bob Bolton's bellowing summons and knew she had a good thirty seconds before the next sonic boom. The second one was always a little louder, a bit more impatient, and included her full name.

"Rebecca Chandler!" he shouted above the din. He was ten seconds early. Rebecca sighed and clicked the mouse to save her document.

"What now?" she said, glaring at him from his office doorway.

Bob Bolton was perched in his usual editorial position—leaning back in his leather desk chair, his chubby fingers laced behind his bald head. The middle button on his wrinkled, white, short-sleeved shirt was undone as usual. Bob's "uniform," as the newsroom crew referred to his wardrobe behind his back, also consisted of socks that collected in rolls around his ankles, scuffed loafers, and any variety of gray pants. He was loud and boisterous, and loved to lord over the newsroom like a prison warden. He prided himself on being able to see every cubicle from his well-positioned mahogany desk. For Rebecca, his gruff manner no longer cut any ice. She could see past his nail-eating drill sergeant exterior. Bob hated that. Nevertheless, he played the part for fear he'd lose control over his beloved *Indianapolis Sentinel* staff.

"So, I heard you had an encounter with the Beard Bandit today," Bob said. "How many does that make?"

"Seventeen," Rebecca sniped.

"Wanna tell me about it?" Bob asked.

"Not particularly. But I will." Bob raised his bushy eyebrows in response as she continued, "It was quite exciting, actually. I was standing on a corner in Lockerbie Square talking to a Salvation Army Santa. His name was Edwin. He's working his way through architectural school and was kinda cute—"

"Cut to the chase, Chandler. My arteries are hardening."

"The chase. Yes, well, I was engaged in my riveting interview with Edwin when a hooded skateboarder appeared, seemingly out of thin air, snatched the beard from Santa's chin and then darted away into holiday traffic without so much as a glance backward."

"And you just stood there?" Bob questioned.

"At first, yes," Rebecca fired back. "Then I gave chase and was nearly hit by a Toyota minivan."

"So you let him get away," Bob barked, ignoring the minivan part.

"No, Bob, I darted out into traffic, ran across the tops of half a dozen cars Jackie Chan-style, tackled the kid and disabled him with a swift but lethal blow to the neck. Street-corner Santas all over the city are hailing me a hero."

"Okay. Okay," Bob sighed. "Tell me you at least got a good look at him."

"He was wearing a hood."

Bob rubbed his chin as if deep in thought. "Seventeen victims . . . what's this punk trying to prove, anyway?"

Rebecca shrugged, already bored with this conversation. "I dunno. Maybe Santa forgot to bring him the BB gun he wanted when he was ten and he has lingering issues."

Bob sniffed at her attempt at humor and took a sip from his Indiana Hoosiers coffee mug. "Well, stay on it. Whoever this kid is, he's selling papers. Maybe when he decides to come in from the cold, you can get him to turn himself in to you. Something like that happened to that beat reporter for the *Telegraph* last year."

"Yes, but that was a serial killer. This kid swipes fake beards."

Bob cleared the phlegm from his throat and began shuffling the papers on his desk. Rebecca recognized the telltale signs. "Let me guess. The Beard Bandit isn't the real reason you called me in here. Is it?"

Bob gave her his best "I-don't-know-what-you're-talking-about" face, and then, when he saw Rebecca wasn't buying it, slipped into a sheepish grin. "All right, you got me."

"What is it this time, Bob?" she sighed.

"Rebecca, did I mention how much I enjoyed your story about the three-legged dog last month? You know, the one that saved the old lady from the fire. You write with such warmth and sincerity."

"Uh oh," Rebecca said, her radar on full alert. A compliment from Bob Bolton could only mean one thing. "What do you want, Bob?"

"Want?" Bob said, feigning innocence.

"Well, the last time you called me in here to butter me up I ended up spending Independence Day with America's oldest living veteran."

"And turned in some of your best work, I might add."

Rebecca fixed him with a defiant glare. "Bob, it was beyond pathetic. He was a hundred and four. He had no idea where he was and every time a firecracker went off, he started looking for a foxhole." Bob snorted as if he found this mildly amusing. "When do I get to be a real reporter?" Rebecca asked finally, her voice dropping to avoid her coworkers' curious ears.

Bob edged forward. She'd just entered his discomfort zone. "Soon," he assured her. "I'm grooming you."

"You've been saying that since you had hair," Rebecca retorted, no longer caring who heard her. "I'm tired of just covering the feature fluff. I want something with teeth. Give me a real assignment."

Bob leaned back in his chair, his eyes narrowing, his demeanor shifting from uncomfortable to suspicious in an instant. "So, you think you know it all now, eh? And features are beneath you. Is that it?"

Rebecca sighed heavily. She was losing patience.

"No, Bob. I just want to feel like my talents are being appreciated, that's all."

"I appreciate your talents," Bob said defensively. "Did I ever tell you how much I appreciate your willingness to work holidays?"

Rebecca winced. Bob had buried the lead. "The answer is no," she said firmly.

"Wait, what's the question?" Bob said, again dipping into his acting reservoir.

"You were about to ask me to sacrifice my Christmas . . . again," Rebecca shot back, heading him off at the pass.

"I was?" Bob made one last attempt before giving up and grinning like a used-car salesman. "Okay. I was. But not just for any old story. This one's really special—a perennial favorite."

"Let me guess," Rebecca said. "The candle-lighting ceremony in the park?"

"Nope," Bob said, enjoying her little guessing game. "Even better. Think—readers' favorite."

"The snowman-building competition," Rebecca fired back, sure she'd nailed it this time.

"No. Think heartwarming, life-affirming—a real tearjerker," Bob said.

"The Hell's Angels Toy Drive." Bob gleefully shook his head. "I give up," she said, enjoying how her boss sagged in disappointment that the game was over.

"Hamden, Indiana," he said finally. "Ring any bells?"

"Not Secret Santa," she said, with as much disdain as she could muster.

"That's the one."

"Bob, that story's so tired I'm getting sleepy just thinking about it."

Bob raised his eyebrows in disbelief. "Not according to our readership," he defended. "Year in and year out, Secret Santa is our most popular holiday story."

Rebecca checked her watch, hoping the hint would do the trick, but Bob would have none of it.

"Every Christmas Eve, a mysterious stranger appears out of the mist to bestow a gift on some poor, less fortunate sap," he said, now up out of his chair and into full selling mode. "Readers eat that stuff up."

"That's funny," Rebecca said with a smirk. "It gives me indigestion."

"I've already slated it for the feature front, Christmas Day," Bob said, sitting on the edge of his desk. "Naturally, I want my best reporter on the job."

Rebecca glared at him, hoping her expression alone

would be a sufficient answer. But she could tell from the look in his eyes—he wasn't about to budge. "Spare me, Bob. The real reason you want me is because I'm single, and you assume I have nothing better to do for the holidays than spend it in some podunk town in the middle of nowhere."

"I'll up your per diem to thirty bucks," Bob bargained. "And I'll throw in one of my wife's rum cakes."

Rebecca had heard enough. "Forget it. I couldn't care less who got a new oxygen tank in their stocking and—despite what you might think, I *do* have plans this Christmas. Ryan is taking his 'fiancée' to Maui."

"Anybody I know?" Bob asked, in a feeble attempt at humor.

"Very funny," she replied tersely. "He plans to pop the question soon. I can feel it. And when he does, I will hesitate for an appropriate period of time—say ten seconds—and then give him a resounding *Yes!*"

"Okay, Chandler, I'll cut you a break," Bob responded. "But don't come crying to me when Winstead wins the Pulitzer for the Secret Santa story."

"Aloha," Rebecca said, exiting his office with a triumphant smile.

CHAPTER 2

Ryan Corbin had waltzed into Rebecca's life by accident. Literally. It was at the corner coffee shop, Churchill Grounds, where Rebecca stopped every morning on her way to the office. On the fateful morning their paths collided, Rebecca was in a rush, ready to face the day's deadline. Ryan was coming through the door when she was going out. The next thing she knew, he was wearing her decaf espresso all over the front of his Armani suit. Rebecca braced herself for the inevitable meltdown but—to her surprise—he handled it all with graceful aplomb and good humor.

Their first date was four hours later. Lunch at Chianti's—the cozy Italian eatery that would become "their place." They shared a window table for two that looked out on the charming Broad Ripple Village, and listened to the soothing sounds of an ex–department store piano player plunk out Burt Bacharach tunes for tips. By the time the salad arrived, Rebecca had fallen in love.

Eighteen months, three weeks and two days later, Rebecca was still waiting for a commitment.

Christmas was two weeks away, and Ryan had been dropping hints like hand grenades. He'd commented on the size of her fingers, how they seemed to be about the same as his sister Diana's. At Thanksgiving dinner, he'd picked up a china saucer and checked the bottom for the brand and, on a stroll through the promenade the previous weekend, he'd paused for a full two minutes to look in the window at Baby Gap.

But despite those encouraging signs, Rebecca was reluctant to get her hopes up. She'd been burned too many times before. But when Ryan informed her rather matter-of-factly that he was taking her to Maui for Christmas, Rebecca felt a charge of optimism. Maybe, just maybe, the moment had finally arrived.

Waiting in the mile-long, preholiday post office line, Rebecca thought about her future. Maybe she would quit her job, tell Bob to find himself another flunky to do his sappy fluff pieces. She would be a stay-at-home wife to a successful investment banker husband. Maybe she'd write a book, get involved with some charity work or head up the symphony guild. She could host a weekly poetry reading in her parlor and sit around with her fellow social-climbing friends sipping tea, comparing plastic surgeons and pseudo-intellectualizing over the words of Deepak Chopra and James Redfield.

"You're next," a woman behind her urged impatiently. Jolted back to reality, Rebecca gave her a sarcastic "Thanks." Not even the post office could ruin her mood today.

But by the time she arrived at the Christmas tree lot, insecurity had set in and the cynical Rebecca had returned. What if she were imagining all this? What if Ryan had no intention of proposing to her? What if Maui were just a vacation to assuage his guilt? A ploy to keep her at bay for six more months?

The lot was nearly empty except for a few scrawny rejects that looked as if they'd fallen off the back of the truck. Rebecca studied the leftovers. "That one's on sale for fifty dollars," a lot attendant bargained.

"Fifty bucks! For that twig!" Rebecca protested.

"Take it or leave it, lady," he said gruffly. Rebecca sighed and reached for her purse.

With the scrawny tree strapped to the roof of her broken-down VW Beetle, Rebecca chugged up to her modest single-story house. She was struggling to untie the tree when the rope suddenly gave way and sent her falling backward onto the ground with a thump. There, she watched helplessly as her new Christmas tree slid off the back of her car and hit the driveway with a crack. Another branch had bitten the dust. She glanced across the street at her neighbor's house. It looked like a cover for *Exquisite Homes* magazine. The shimmering white lights were perfectly aligned, strung along the gutters, draped over the bushes, and wrapped around the trunks of their majestic trees. Through the large bay window an eight-foot spruce was a glowing testament to holiday cheer. Rebecca could almost smell the cookies baking in the oven in anticipation of the well-dressed guests that were no doubt on the way over. Then she looked over at her sole lawn decoration—the plastic Rudolph she'd gotten on sale at Wal-Mart was now missing a leg.

Inside, Rebecca hung the too-heavy ornaments on the flimsy branches of her tree. She thought about Ryan and wondered why she sometimes doubted his sincerity. Maybe she had been a reporter too long. Cynicism had taken over, and now she had a hard time believing in anything. Just as she grabbed a handful of tinsel, the phone rang. She practically snatched it from the cradle.

Her shoulders sagged when she heard the voice on the other end. "Oh, hi Sue," Rebecca said, trying not to sound disappointed. Then the guilt set in and she spent the next few minutes convincing her sister the lack of enthusiasm in her voice was unintended, that she was just tired and had been expecting a call from Ryan, who was missing in action.

Rebecca was certain that her younger sibling had taken a special course on how to push her buttons. Susan lived in Columbus with her computer parts sales rep husband, Michael, and their three straight-A Stepford kids, all of whom played at least two instruments and spoke a foreign language. They were a living, breathing centerfold for *Family Circle,* and they annoyed

Rebecca to no end. However, she did her best to play the role of the dutiful aunt, especially on birthdays and at Christmastime. But the fact of the matter was, if she found herself in their presence for any length of time, she'd break out into a rash and start slurring her words.

Sue was the type of person who always spoke with an undercurrent. She meant well, but she had long ago mastered the art of passive-aggressive and never knew when to leave well enough alone. What's more, she seemed to relish lording her life of domestic bliss over Rebecca's head. Apparently Sue had found the pot of gold at the end of life's rainbow, and Rebecca had gotten a bag of coal.

"Of course I want to see you guys this Christmas," Rebecca fibbed, mentally chastising herself for not spending the extra few cents and getting caller ID. "But I just don't see how I can possibly swing it. Ryan is taking me to Maui." Sue continued her onslaught, mortified at the thought of a tropical Christmas. "Sue, I know Maui is not traditional in your book, but think of it this way: While you're snowbound in fifteen-degree weather, I'll be digging my toes in the warm sand and sipping an umbrella drink." Rebecca listened as her sister turned to inform the room of Aunt Becka's plans. "Look, Sis. Your house is always full of screaming kids. You won't even know I'm not—" A call-waiting beep interrupted Rebecca's train of thought. "Sue, I've got a call coming in. We'll argue later." Rebecca clicked over, and a smile immediately spread across her face. It was Ryan.

"Your timing's impeccable," she said with a lilt in her voice. "I was on with my sister, Susie Homemaker. So, where are you anyway?"

Rebecca listened patiently as Ryan related his traveler's tale of woe. He was stuck in Chicago—all the outbound flights had been canceled due to a winter storm. The hotels were filling up fast, and he was going to try to find a room.

"You're kidding," Rebecca said, the light fading out of her face. "I was hoping I'd see you tonight."

"Sweetheart, I'm sorry," Ryan apologized. "It's beyond my control. But if it's any consolation, I have something in my pocket that might just make it worth the wait."

Rebecca brightened. She could practically picture the ring box. "Ryan, don't do this to me. You know I hate surprises."

"Oh, I have a feeling you'll like this one," Ryan teased.

Rebecca flushed. "You wouldn't consider giving me a little hint, would you?"

A man waiting for the phone cleared his throat loudly. "Not a chance, babe. But if you meet me at Chianti's tomorrow evening, you can see for yourself."

"How about seven?" Rebecca gushed.

"Perfect," Ryan said. "Look, I have to go find a hotel. I'll call you later. Love you."

"Love you too," she said and then he was gone. Her hope renewed, Rebecca fell back on the couch, a dreamy look on her face. She glanced at her sagging tree and giggled. Suddenly, it was worthy of Rockefeller Center.

CHAPTER 3

No restaurant in Indy was as charming as Chianti's at night. The gas fireplace burned beneath a mantel festively decorated with boughs of pine and holly. In the corner, a frosted Christmas tree glimmered with white lights that reflected off the strands of silver tinsel. The usual piano player was at his post, but the strains of Bacharach had given way to holiday favorites. Despite her usual aversion to silly seasonal tunes, Rebecca was in such a good mood she actually found them somewhat charming. Everything seemed perfect. She stared out the restaurant window, watching and waiting in anticipation for her prince to arrive. Soon, his silver chariot would pull to the curb and he'd emerge. She'd watch him, a whimsical smile on her face as he took the ticket from the valet and retrieved his long camel overcoat from the backseat. She'd spy on him as he put it on, and then wait for him to turn toward the window and see her. He'd know just where to look because this was their spot, their table, their place. This is where their relationship began and where, on this magical night, it would move forward.

Yes, tonight, this would be the setting for the making of a memory—a moment they would cherish for a lifetime.

"Excuse me, signorina. Is everything all right?"

Rebecca looked up into the smiling face of the waiter. "Of course," Rebecca said. "Why wouldn't it be?"

"No reason," he said gently. "It's just that you've been waiting for over an hour. Are you sure I can't get you something?"

"Oh no," Rebecca said. "I'm fine. He should be here any minute. He's flying in from Chicago, assuming he was able to get a flight, what with the weather and all," she overexplained. The waiter nodded and retreated, and Rebecca turned back to the window. Maybe he was right. Maybe she should be concerned. She decided she'd try to occupy herself. She tore open a cold roll and started memorizing the menu. Where could Ryan possibly be?

Hours later, she watched as the last couple drove off from the lonely curb. The valet turned toward the window, meeting her eye for a moment as if to say: "Let's go lady. I wanna get home to my family." Rebecca checked her watch again and her heart sank. She picked up her cell phone and tried calling again. Still no answer.

"Signorina, perhaps he was detained," the waiter said, breaking Rebecca's troubled trance. She smiled up at him, doing her best to hold it together when what she really wanted was to bury her head into his shoulder and cry her eyes out.

She rationalized instead. "You know what I think happened? There was probably some old lady who was desperate to get back to her dying husband's side. So Ryan, soft touch that he is, gave up his seat. And, since he couldn't recharge his cell phone, he wasn't able to call me."

The waiter nodded, seamlessly slipping into Rebecca's self-deluding fantasy. "And, no doubt, the lines in Chicago were probably down—due to the storm—so he couldn't even use a pay phone."

"Right," Rebecca chimed in, grateful for his help. "Or maybe he slipped on the ice . . . and hit his head. And—"

The waiter jumped in. "And he was probably knocked out for a while and then he—"

"Woke up with amnesia!" Rebecca finished. "He probably stumbled around lost, bleeding from the head and muttering my name."

"Tragic," the waiter said sympathetically.

"But then something triggered his memory. A song on the radio. A whiff of my perfume on a passerby. And suddenly he remembered who he was and how much he loved me. I'm sure he's rushing to get here as fast as he can. When he finally does show up, he'll be carrying this big, beautiful bouquet of—" Rebecca looked out the window and stopped midsentence. What she saw took her breath away like a skinny-dip in a cold mountain pond. "Flowers," she finished, dreamily. Ryan was outside—holding the most beautiful roses she'd ever seen.

"Perhaps you should go to him," the waiter encouraged.

"Perhaps," Rebecca echoed wistfully.

"Hello, Rebecca," Ryan said as she approached him. "These are for you."

Something was off-kilter in his body language, an edge to his voice, but all Rebecca could see at that moment was the bouquet now cradled in her arms. Everything would be okay. Whatever his reasons for keeping her waiting, she would accept his apology. Tomorrow it would all be forgotten.

"These are to apologize," he said, referring to the flowers. "Were you waiting long?"

Rebecca glared at him as if to say "How could you ask such a question?" But she bit her tongue. Something in his face disarmed her. He seemed distracted. She hoped it was merely his guilt for being late, but the knot in her stomach told her otherwise. "Not really," she finally replied. "Just since seven. Three hours and ... twenty-one minutes. Give or take."

"I'm really sorry," Ryan said in his beaten puppy dog voice. "I was detained in Chicago."

"You mean, by the airport police?" Rebecca retorted, determined to lighten the mood.

Ryan chuckled a little too energetically. "Not exactly. Actually, it's a very interesting story. If you were a writer, it'd make a great movie."

"I am a writer," Rebecca replied.

"I mean . . . a real writer," Ryan said, not meaning to be cruel but stinging her ego nevertheless. "You see," he continued slowly, his story stumbling out of the gate. "This is difficult . . ."

"Sweetheart, you know you can tell me anything," Rebecca said, trying to disguise the irritation in her voice.

Ryan nodded twice, took a deep breath and let flow. "You see, I'm stranded at the airport for four hours— not a cab to be found. I decide I need some air, so I step out to the curb, and suddenly . . . this car pulls up. A woman leans over and asks me if flight number 714 has come in. I tell her I'm pretty sure that flight's been canceled and probably won't be in until morning. She asks me if I needed a ride and I say sure . . . hoping she can drop me off at a hotel."

"Ryan, where is this going?" Rebecca asked, suspiciously.

Ryan continued as if he didn't hear the question. "Well, we end up driving around for hours—from hotel to hotel—and there isn't a room to be had. But, Nina never complains and is just so . . . nice about the whole thing."

24

"Nina?" Rebecca said, the knot in her stomach constricting.

"Finally," Ryan blurted out, as if his story was just some jolly anecdote shared at the office Christmas party, "she offered me a spot on her couch for the night, and by that time I was so exhausted . . . I said . . . yes."

Rebecca had heard enough. "Bottom line me, Ryan."

"We made love," he said, sheepishly.

Rebecca's heart leapt to her throat. She waited for the punch line, the cockeyed smile to tip her off to the cruel joke. Then she would let him know, in no uncertain terms, just how unfunny she thought his little jest was, and then she'd be mad at him for a couple of hours, maybe three. He'd feel terrible, admit it was in bad taste and then bend over backward to make it up to her. Everything would be all right. Life would go on as planned.

"But I don't want you to think it was just some cheap, physical thing," Ryan said, lowering his eyes. Rebecca was vaguely aware that his mouth was still moving. She did her best to focus. "We made a real connection, Becka. It was as if fate had, by some strange coincidence, brought us together at that moment in time."

"For a one-night stand!" Rebecca blurted out, her trance now shattered.

"That's what I'm trying to tell you," Ryan said. "It was so much more. It was more like a . . . magical . . . sharing of souls."

"Ryan, you're supposed to be 'sharing your soul' with me," Rebecca fired back.

Ryan moved in closer to her, as if to seek her understanding, and then confessed, "We love each other, Rebecca," he said.

"We? You mean you and me?" Rebecca asked, hopefully.

"No . . . Nina and me," Ryan said, softly correcting her. "We are soul mates. I know it sounds crazy but—"

"Crazy?" Rebecca said, cutting him off. "Daffy Duck is crazy. This is Hannibal Lecter!"

"Look, we don't expect you to understand," Ryan said, his voice so patronizing it was all she could do to keep from slugging him.

"We? You're already a *we!*" Rebecca shrieked. "We weren't a *we* for at least five months after *we* started dating."

"But that's just it," Ryan said. "This isn't dating. This is a connection. We're soul—"

"Soul mates! I heard you the first time," Rebecca interrupted, her bewilderment quickly turning to anger. "Well, at the risk of raining on your little two-timing parade—let me give you a news flash: You have to have a soul . . . before you can mate it!" Rebecca tossed the flowers at him and stalked over to the valet.

"Rebecca, wait!" Ryan called after her. "Don't go like this! I know it may hurt now . . . but it'll get easier with time. Trust me."

CHAPTER 4

I hate Christmas," Rebecca muttered to herself, sitting alone in her darkened living room, surrounded by an entire box of used Kleenex. No Ryan. No trip to Maui. And, in front of her, the most pathetic tree known to man. Christmas, the relentless season, had let her down once again.

"Jeez, what happened to you?" Bob asked the next morning when Rebecca stepped into his office, her eyes puffed up like a blowfish. "You look like you slept in a dumpster."

"My life is a dumpster," Rebecca muttered as she

slumped into the chair across from his desk. "Ryan 'met' someone."

Bob leaned back and loosened his tie, doing his best to suppress a smirk. "You're kidding."

"Getting dumped is not a subject I usually joke about," Rebecca said dryly.

"So, I guess Maui's off, huh?" Bob said without even a trace of sensitivity.

Rebecca glared a hole through him, too deflated to muster a witty rejoinder. "Try not to sound so happy about it."

"Sorry." Bob retreated. "Is there anything I can do?"

"No. I'm here to inform you that I no longer have a life and that I will work on Christmas just like every other year."

"And Secret Santa?" Bob said, his eyes lighting up with renewed hope.

Rebecca sighed. "Sure, why not. Let's just complete my humiliation." Bob did his best to mask his jubilation. "But let's get one thing straight," Rebecca continued. "If I must waste my time on this stupid story, I intend to do it my way."

"Which means?" Bob said, arching his eyebrows.

"You give me the chance to prove to you that I'm a real reporter."

"Okay . . . ," he hesitated, awaiting her proposal.

"I want to unmask him."

Bob tapped a pencil on his desk as he contemplated her proposal. *"Reveal* the Secret Santa?"

Rebecca nodded. "Yep. I'll do an investigative piece. Leave no stone unturned. Refuse to take no for an answer. And any other cliché you can think of. I'll flush that sucker out like a rabid bird dog. And, after I'm done, he'll be known as the bleeding heart do-gooder, formerly known as Secret Santa."

Bob gazed off at the ceiling, deep in thought, as if he were deciding whether or not to unplug his favorite aunt from the ventilator. When he looked back at Rebecca, she could tell he'd bought it.

"I've got a pair of Pacers tickets that says you can't do it," he challenged. "Courtside."

Rebecca leaned across his desk and thrust out her hand. "You're on."

Rebecca's trusty Volkswagen had seemed an unwilling participant ever since she rolled out of her driveway that morning. Now, somewhere in the middle of nowhere, her engine sounded as if it would spontaneously combust at any moment. She flipped on the radio to drown out the noise, only to find a nauseating array of Christmas tunes. "Bah humbug," she mumbled and switched it off. Why on earth would she want to listen to some old man crooning about an outcast reindeer with a radioactive nose?

She looked out at the surrounding countryside and wondered what would possess anyone to live in the middle of a cornfield. Come to think of it, she hadn't seen a road sign for the last twenty minutes. Could she have taken a wrong turn? How would she ever find her way back to civilization? Wasn't this the kind of place where UFOs landed and took hostages? She pulled the wrinkled road map from the visor above her head, spread it out across the steering wheel and tried to navigate. "Go west on Route 41, 'til it ends, turn right, go five miles . . . right again." When she looked up, all she could see was a collage of black and white looming in front of her. She screamed a word that would make her dead grandmother blush and slammed on the brakes, narrowly missing the Jersey cow standing in the middle of the road.

She dropped her head to the wheel and let out a

long, drawn-out groan. Then her engine coughed four times and died. When she finally looked up again, the cow was standing there glaring at her like she was the star of some circus freak show. "What are you staring at?" she grumbled as she tried to restart her car. She tried again and then again. Not so much as a false start. Her precious little bug was dead on arrival.

"Ryan, I will never forgive you for this," Rebecca said. As she got out of the car, she was engulfed by white smoke that smoldered out of the tiny engine. "Oh, this is just getting better and better," she said, fighting back an emotional meltdown. The cow mooed. "Oh, shut up!" she barked, as she whipped out her cell phone and dialed 411. "Hamden, Indiana," she said impatiently. "The number for a service station— with road service."

CHAPTER 5

Hamden, Indiana, looked like a Currier and Ives Christmas postcard. Quaint shop windows were adorned with toy trains and miniature skating scenes. Light posts were wrapped with red ribbons, strands of white lights lined the roofs of the buildings, and a drooping banner hanging over Main Street trumpeted the annual "Christmas Pageant, Saturday night." At the center of the square was a gazebo where a young couple snuggled together and shared a cup of hot cocoa.

Rebecca saw it all through the passenger window of

a big white tow truck and it made her sick. As far as she was concerned, she'd just entered the gates of holiday purgatory.

Sitting behind the wheel was a pot-bellied yokel named Harley. He had been jawing nonstop since he'd picked her up on the highway. By the time they'd reached downtown Hamden, he'd managed to relate at least a dozen stories about distressed motorists. Rebecca secretly wished that she was a spy—not that she liked danger, but she'd heard that they kept tiny cyanide tablets on hand in case they found themselves at a point of no return. Rebecca had reached such a crossroads. She glanced at the side mirror and caught a glimpse of her lonely Beetle being dragged helplessly along.

"Yes, ma'am," Harley piped up, a big grin on his face. "On the surface, Hamden's not much to look at. But we do have something the big city is sorely lacking."

Rebecca turned glumly toward him. "And what is that, Harley? Free parking?"

"Christmas," Harley responded, like a little kid displaying his first lost tooth.

"Excuse me, but I thought Christmas was sort of a . . . universal phenomenon," Rebecca replied, determined to quash his exuberance.

"Not here," said Harley, undeterred. "We do Christmas right. Here, it's sort of a year-round thing."

"Sounds exhausting."

"I don't mean we have decorations and caroling all year. I'm talking about the spirit."

"Oh, the spirit," Rebecca said, with thinly veiled sarcasm. "Speaking of the Christmas spirit, what can you tell me about . . . Secret Santa?"

Harley chuckled and shook his head, and Rebecca could tell that another story was percolating. "It was Christmas '95. My business was in the toilet, if you'll pardon the expression. Just not enough car trouble in Hamden. But I knew that just beyond those cornfields was a big, beautiful highway where folks like yourself were breaking down all the time. All I needed was a way to bring them to me. Secret Santa showed me the way."

"I give up. How?" Rebecca shrugged.

Harley looked over at her and winked. "By putting the tow in my truck," he said, proudly.

"Secret Santa bought you a tow truck?" Rebecca said, her eyes narrowing.

"No—a hydraulic lift," Harley clarified.

"So, any ideas who he might be?"

Harley waved at a passerby. "Oh, I have my theories. But, to tell you the truth, I'm not so sure I wanna know. It's more fun this way."

Rebecca flashed him her best painted-on smile. Fun was the last thing on her mind. "Okay, if you *did* wanna know—who would you guess?"

Harley scratched his chin, as if considering the question for the first time. "I reckon ... if I had to wager a guess ... I'd lay my money on ... Mr. John Martin Carter."

Rebecca slipped her miniature notebook and pencil out of her pocket with one expert flick of her wrist. "And, who might he be?"

"Only the richest man in town," Harley trumpeted.

Rebecca scribbled the name down and underlined it twice. John Martin Carter had just moved to the top of the suspect list.

A few minutes later, Rebecca arrived via tow truck at the steps of the Olde Hamden Inn. Under more pleasant circumstances, she might have considered its old-style Victorian elegance and wraparound porch charming. If Ryan were with her, maybe. She suddenly had a vision of herself on the sands of Waikiki sipping a drink out of a pineapple-shaped mug as Ryan slowly rubbed her back with coconut tanning oil.

Instead, there she stood with a grease monkey named Harley.

Harley grabbed her bags and led the way inside. At the front desk, he tapped the bell with such relish that it practically welded Rebecca's teeth together. Seconds later, an impish little lady emerged from the back room.

"I brought you a customer, Winiford. She's a reporter from the city," Harley announced, as if he had just delivered Queen Elizabeth.

"Why, welcome to Hamden," she said. "I'm the innkeeper, Winiford Callaway."

"Hi," Rebecca said tersely. "I'd like a room."

"Oh, I'm so sorry, dear. I rented our last room just ten minutes ago to a couple by the name of . . . Bird."

"You know what they say," Harley said. Rebecca looked at him, wondering what was coming next.

"The early bird gets the worm." Harley laughed, impressed with his own wit, "or in this case the room."

Winiford couldn't help but chuckle herself. "Harley, where do you come up with such things?"

"Oh, I don't know. They just seem to pop out of me sometimes."

"Excuse me," Rebecca said, "but is there anywhere *else* to stay in this town?"

Winiford straightened up quickly, realizing this was no time for frivolity. "Well, we do have a place that takes our guests in the event of an overflow," she offered.

"Great," Rebecca said with a relieved sigh. "Just point me in the right direction."

"Harley, why don't you take Miss . . ."

"Chandler. Rebecca Chandler."

" . . . Miss Chandler over to Corapeake Cove. I'll call ahead and let Russell know you're coming."

"Sure thing," Harley piped up.

"Corapeake Cove?" Rebecca mused. "Sounds charming."

Less than ten minutes later, Harley's truck rolled onto the serene grounds of Corapeake Cove and stopped just in front of a sign that read, Corapeake Cove Rest Home. The place screamed "old people" in every direction. There were bird feeders and angel statues everywhere. The long brick building was plain as melba toast and about as inviting as a summer vacation in Death Valley.

"You've got to be kidding me!" Rebecca blurted out.

"No ma'am," Harley replied. "The rest home always takes the overflow when the inn is full." Rebecca gave him her most incredulous look. "Hey, it's not so bad," he assured her. "The food's good and they have some pretty mean bingo games on Thursday nights."

Rebecca wrinkled her brow and resigned herself. "Please tell me you'll have my car ready by tomorrow."

"No sweat, Miss Chandler," he assured her. "I'm the best mechanic in town."

"Aren't you the only mechanic in town?"

"That too."

Rebecca shook her head, opened the door and slid out of the front seat. She pulled her suitcase out of the back of the truck and then watched like a concerned mother as Harley drove away, towing her poor little sick car behind. When he was out of sight, Rebecca turned toward the rest home and let out an exasperated sigh. The day that couldn't possibly get any worse just had.

From the moment she stumbled into the front door, Rebecca felt awkward and out of place. She considered just turning around and leaving. Maybe she could get out before anybody saw her. But her escape was thwarted.

"Evenin', miss. Would you like a cookie?"

Rebecca turned toward the voice and found herself face-to-face with a tall, handsome black man. He had a kind face with gentle eyes and appeared to be in his late fifties. He was holding a half-empty tray of chocolate chip cookies. "No, thank you," Rebecca replied. "I came from the Olde Hamden Inn."

"Oh, yes," he said, a welcoming smile on his face. "Winiford said you'd be needing a place to stay. My name's Russell."

"Rebecca Chandler."

He put the cookie tray down, picked up her suitcase, and gestured for her to follow him.

"You know, I had no idea Hamden was such a tourist hotspot," Rebecca said, as she followed Russell down the dreary corridor.

"Most times no. But we do have a lot of seasonal visitors. They come here looking for the Christmas spirit. We have the best live pageant in the whole state of Indiana."

"Is that right?"

"Yes, ma'am. A few years back, Mr. Carter donated the money for sets and costumes."

"Would that be . . . Mr. John Martin Carter?" Rebecca asked, her interest piqued.

"Oh, you know Mr. Carter?" Russell asked.

"Not yet," Rebecca said slyly.

Rebecca had to smile when she saw the tiny room.

The hospital bed was made up with flowered sheets and a baby blue spread. In the corner, a television hung from the ceiling. And a shiny bed pan was perched on the dresser like an oversized ashtray. Russell put her suitcase down on a luggage rack and pulled open the curtains. Rebecca stepped to the window and looked out on the backyard where a stone path wound through a garden of boxwoods and pine trees. There was a small lily pond too, with a miniature wooden bridge that arched across the water. The perfect setting . . . to die, she mused to herself.

"It's not the Waldorf, but it's cozy," Russell said, as he adjusted the thermostat.

"If you're of the mind, there's bingo in the recreation room at seven," Russell announced. "And—afterward—we all gather in front of the television for *Touched By an Angel* reruns."

Rebecca felt her stomach growl and remembered she hadn't eaten anything since breakfast. "Actually, I was wondering where I could get something to eat around here."

"I'm sorry to say we finished up dinner at four-thirty," Russell said, apologetically. "Town square's a short walk, though. You might try Charlie's Diner."

"Oh, and one more thing. You wouldn't happen to have a DSL line, would you? Or any high speed internet access?"

"No, but we do have oxygen hookups in every room . . . if that helps," he mused.

Rebecca gave him a tight smile. Apparently everybody in Hamden was a comedian.

Russell nodded and then pulled the door shut, leaving Rebecca alone. She looked around at her surroundings and let out an exasperated sigh. "Perfect. In less than twenty-four hours, I've lost my fiancé, my car, and my dignity. Now, I'm gonna go to sleep in an old folks' home. Welcome to the Twilight Zone."

She climbed into the mechanical bed and played with the buttons for a few minutes. Head up, feet down. Feet up. Head down. She flicked on the overhead television, muted the sound and flipped around the channels. When she came to a travel documentary on Hawaii she sighed and flicked off the set. As she turned her light out, she noticed the light in the room across the hall was still on. From her vantage point, Rebecca could glimpse the white hair of a woman, sitting up in bed, reading.

She wondered what growing old would be like. Rebecca closed her eyes and tried to block it out of her mind. The last thing she remembered before drifting off to sleep was the sound of a grandfather clock striking eleven.

When Rebecca opened her eyes the next morning, she wasn't sure where she was, but when she sat up and looked around, it all came back to her. This wasn't a nightmare after all. Yesterday had actually happened.

She dressed quickly, anxious to tackle her story and more anxious to escape this geriatric quagmire.

The dining room was teeming with elderly residents as she walked through. She spotted Russell carrying a tray of styrofoam cups, and he nodded to her. "Morning, Rebecca. How'd you sleep?"

"Fine. Thank you."

"Would you like some juice?"

"Why not?" Rebecca said, "I could use a little pick-me-up." She selected a cup, took a sip and suddenly gagged. "What is this?" she choked. "It tastes like liquid fish eggs."

"Prune juice," he said with a twinkle. "Keeps a body regular."

As Russell continued to the next table, Rebecca eye-balled a bowl of mints. She scooped up a fistful, shoved them into her mouth to kill the taste and then rushed to catch up to Russell.

"You missed a doozy of a bingo match last evening. Miss Ruthie won a seventeen dollar pot on the final card," he said, nodding toward a rather feisty-looking old lady holding court at the head table.

"My loss," Rebecca said, plucking a postcard out of her purse. "Before I forget, would you mind dropping this in your outgoing mail?"

Russell took it from her and smiled. "Be happy to."

"My sister worries when she doesn't know where I am," Rebecca explained.

Russell looked down at the card and noticed the palm trees and surf scene. "But this is a postcard from Hawaii."

"I know," Rebecca said with an impish smile. She headed for the door and then stopped. "Oh, one more thing. Could you tell me where to find Mr. John Martin Carter?"

"Three ninety-one South Madison," Russell said without hesitation. "The big house on the corner. You can't miss it."

The Carter mansion seemed out of place in unassuming Hamden. The house was tucked back from the road, the centerpiece of sprawling grounds made up of evergreen trees, lavish gardens, and bubbling fountains. The house itself was a massive English Tudor, but the white Christmas lights that lined the roof made it somehow seem inviting. Rebecca stepped up to the front gate and pressed the buzzer. No answer. She peered through the iron bars trying to glimpse some sign of life. Nobody. She pressed again. Finally, the speaker crackled with static and then ...

"Carter residence," a male voice said, flatly. "May I help you?"

"Yes," Rebecca said. "I'm here to see Mr. Carter."

"And, your name is ... ?"

"Rebecca Chandler," she said firmly.

"From?" the voice continued.

"The *Indianapolis Sentinel*," Rebecca said, growing impatient. "I'm a reporter."

After a long silence, the voice answered emphatically, "I'm afraid I don't find a Rebecca Chandler on Mr. Carter's appointment log."

"That's probably because ... I don't have an appointment," Rebecca shot back.

"I'm afraid Mr. Carter doesn't see anyone without an appointment," the voice said, with a trace of superiority.

"Well, okay . . . I'd like to make one," Rebecca countered.

"For what time?" the voice asked.

Rebecca checked her watch. "Let's see . . . it's now 10:05. How about 10:15?"

"I'm sorry, but Mr. Carter is not available," the voice said, with a tone of finality.

"Okay, when will he be—?" Rebecca was still mid-sentence when the intercom clicked off abruptly.

From Carter's house it was a short six blocks to the town square. Along the way, Rebecca strolled through modest Hamden neighborhoods with white picket fences and houses decked out for the holidays. She found herself curious about the small town lives the residents here must lead, the kind of existence where everybody knows everybody else's business, and you can't even go to the market without bumping into somebody who'd seen you naked in sixth grade PE.

CHAPTER 6

The town square was teeming with rosy-cheeked shoppers when Rebecca arrived. For a moment she watched them scurry about in their hats and gloves and scarves, popping in and out of stores in search of the ultimate Christmas gift. In the middle of the row of stores, Rebecca found a rather drab-looking brick office with a large front window and a hand-painted sign that read: "Hamden Herald— Good News for Good People." Below that were the words George Gibson, Editor. Rebecca plucked the day's edition out of the newspaper box by the door and scanned the headlines: "Annual Tree Lighting Tomorrow Night" and "Winiford Callaway to Narrate Pageant."

"Cutting-edge stuff," Rebecca said to herself, as she opened the front door.

A bell jingled as she entered the tiny office. Rebecca looked around, taking in her low-tech surroundings. There wasn't a computer in sight, not a phone bank or receptionist or even a copy machine. There was an old Coca-Cola clock hanging on the wall, and a framed headline, "Hamden Named Indiana's Most Livable Small Town." Behind the counter, a white-haired man sat at a rolltop desk, his fingers clicking away methodically at the keys of an old Remington. He seemed oblivious to the stranger in his presence. It was the phone that finally tore him away from his work.

"Hamden Herald," he growled. Rebecca watched him with increasing curiosity as he plucked a stubby pencil from behind his ear and began taking notes. "Is that right . . . I see . . . well, good," he said. "I'll see that it gets in. Happy Holidays to you too. Bye."

Rebecca cleared her throat to catch his attention.

He turned from his desk as if surprised to find a customer. "Oh, hello, what can I do for you?"

"My name's Rebecca Chandler," she said cheerfully. "I'm a reporter for the *Sentinel*."

"That the *Indianapolis Sentinel?*" he asked with tepid curiosity.

"One and the same," Rebecca smiled.

"Well, welcome to Hamden," he said matter-of-factly, shuffling over to the counter. "I'm George Gibson. Always nice to meet a 'colleague.'"

"Likewise," Rebecca said cordially. "I was wondering if you could help me with a story I'm working on."

"A story? On Hamden?" George asked with a hint of skepticism.

"Sort of," Rebecca said cautiously. "Specifically, Secret Santa."

George broke into a knowing smile. "Oh, yes. You folks run a piece every year on Christmas Day."

"That's right," Rebecca said, happy not to have to explain further.

"Don't normally send a reporter, though," George said, furrowing his brow. "Usually just a phone call."

"Well," Rebecca continued, trying to appeal to his journalistic ethics, "this year we wanted to do it right. So, here I am."

"How can I help you?" he offered.

Rebecca reached for her notebook and quickly reviewed her notes. "Well, let's look at the history of the so-called Secret Santa. Last year, he left a wheelchair for some kid. What was his name ...?"

"Scotty Westbrook," George said without hesitation. "He's eleven. Parents are dead. Lives with his older sister, Callie, who takes care of him."

"And, the year before it was ..."

"Down payment on a double-wide trailer for Tess and Arthur Meyerson, on account of theirs got burned up in an electrical fire. The year before that we had a flood, ruined the church organ. Secret Santa took care of that too. The new one plays the prettiest hymns you ever heard."

"In '99 ... a dishwasher for an old lady name Figgins," Rebecca chimed in from her notes.

"Couldn't wash 'em by hand anymore on account of her arthritis," George explained.

Rebecca flipped the page. "Paid a seventy-five hundred dollar hospital bill for a Mrs. Ethel Wilkins in '98 ..."

"Husband was in ICU before he died. She didn't have insurance."

"Then, there were various gifts," Rebecca said. "A set

of tools for an indigent carpenter . . . braces for a foster child . . . and so on and so on . . ." Rebecca flipped her notebook closed. "Mr. Gibson, I'm sure you know just about everything that goes on in this town. So, you must have some idea who this Secret Santa might be."

George took a deep breath. "Miss Chandler, may I offer you a little friendly advice?"

"Go ahead," Rebecca replied.

"Don't go playing Woodward and Bernstein. Just file your story like every other year. Leave the secret in Secret Santa."

Rebecca flashed her most patronizing smile. "And why should I, Mr. Gibson? I mean, don't we journalists have a duty to our readers?"

"Maybe in the big city," George replied. "But in Hamden we have a duty to each other. And this old newspaper man knows when it's best to leave well enough alone."

Rebecca smiled and put away her notebook. "One more question, Mr. Gibson. Could you tell me where I might find Scotty Westbrook?"

"Amber Street, 420 South." George said matter-of-factly. "It's about five blocks due west."

"Merry Christmas, Mr. Gibson," Rebecca said, as she turned to leave.

"And to you," he replied. As she disappeared, Gibson just shook his head. He'd never much understood city folks.

Callie and Scotty lived in a clapboard house on the south end of town, a world apart from the Carter mansion. In the crackerbox kitchen, Rebecca shared a cup of tea with Callie, a shy, sandy-haired twenty-year-old who looked like she hadn't had a good night's sleep in about a year. She'd been forced into adulthood four years earlier, when her mom and dad were both killed in a car accident. Rebecca listened sympathetically as Callie related the story, careful to keep her voice down so that her little brother Scotty wouldn't overhear.

"So, now I work at the diner," Callie said. "It's a lotta work but I like it. The people are nice and I make pretty good tips."

"Speaking of nice people, what can you tell me about Secret Santa?" Rebecca asked, trying to change the subject.

Callie shifted in her chair and took a sip of her tea. "Well, what do you want to know?"

"Where do you think Scotty's chair came from?" Rebecca asked, her pencil poised.

"All I know is . . . when we woke up Christmas morning, there it was . . . sitting on the front porch. A note was pinned to it. 'From Secret Santa.'"

Rebecca scribbled the quote on her pad. "Miss Westbrook . . ."

"Callie."

"Callie, do you have any idea who might have left it?"

Callie smiled. "I know exactly who left it there."

Rebecca slid forward in her chair, anticipating the moment of truth. "You do?"

"Sure I do," Callie said, sincerely. "It was an angel . . . straight from heaven. A special angel who wanted to help Scotty."

"An angel? Come on, aren't you curious about who that 'angel' might be?"

"Reverend Terry said you shouldn't question angels," Callie replied sincerely.

Rebecca sighed. "Callie, with all due respect to the reverend, don't you think it would be nice to recognize this Secret Santa for his . . . generosity? To show your gratitude?"

"But I do show my gratitude," Callie said. "Every day."

"You do?" Rebecca said, waiting for the punch line.

"Yes, ma'am. I thank him by the way I live my life, by taking care of my little brother and trying to do right by other people. Just the other day . . . at the diner," Callie continued, "a man accidentally left a twenty-dollar bill on a five-dollar tab—and I chased him four blocks to give him his change."

Rebecca sat incredulous. Maybe all the stories about aliens abducting small town yokels weren't so outlandish after all. "Wow," Rebecca said finally, "That's really something."

"So," Callie said, standing up from the table, "wanna meet Scotty?"

Rebecca found Scotty sitting in his wheelchair in front of an easel, thoroughly engrossed in the partially completed watercolor in front of him. The scene depicted Scotty rising high out of his wheelchair to dunk a basketball, a look of pure joy on his eleven-year-old face. Rebecca looked around the tiny room. He had turned it into a shrine to his favorite team, with an autographed basketball on the shelf, posters on the wall, and basketball cards pinned in perfect order on the bulletin board. Sharing the space with his basketball memorabilia were examples of Scotty's artwork, colorful and dramatic watercolors in which Scotty had cast himself as the star, a tiny wheelchair-bound hero accomplishing some great feat of daring.

"Scotty, there's someone here to see you," Callie said, putting her hand on his shoulder.

Scotty gave Rebecca a shy smile.

"Hi, Scotty," Rebecca greeted.

"Hi," he replied cautiously.

"I see you're a Pacers fan." Scotty nodded politely, not sure what to make of the strange lady standing in his space. "So, I bet you saw Reggie knock down that buzzer beater against the Celtics last Saturday," Rebecca added.

Scotty relaxed. She spoke his language. "Nuthin' but net," he said with a smile.

"So, do you think they have a shot to go the distance?"

Scotty wrinkled his forehead as if he was giving the idea serious thought. "Maybe. If they get help in the middle."

Rebecca smiled. "That's what I like. An optimist."

Rebecca stepped over to his wheelchair. "That is def–

initely not your grandmother's wheelchair. What does it do?"

Scotty jumped at the chance to demonstrate. "Just about everything. It's called a 'smart' chair because it comes fully equipped with computerized sensory and navigational capabilities."

"Wow," Rebecca said, duly impressed. Then, she turned her attention to his artwork. "You know, you're good. This shows a lot of imagination. You should be proud."

"I'm going to art school when I'm old enough," he beamed. "Callie says I have talent."

"She's right," Rebecca said. Then she extended her hand, "It was nice meeting you, Scotty. Hope to see you around."

"Are you coming to the tree lighting ceremony?" he asked as she started to go.

Rebecca was taken off guard. "Should I?"

Scotty shrugged. "Only if you want to see me throw the switch."

Rebecca smiled. "Okay. I'll try to make it."

"It must be hard," Rebecca said, as Callie led her to the front door, "being so young, I mean . . . and having so much responsibility."

Callie nodded. "We have a good life. We may not have much, but we have each other."

Rebecca stepped on the porch. "By the way, do you know a John Martin Carter?"

Callie's face lit up with recognition. "Of course. Everybody in Hamden knows Mr. Carter."

"Do you think maybe . . . *he* . . . could be Scotty's anonymous donor?"

Callie shrugged. "Like I said, it was an angel. And—"

"I know," Rebecca finished her thought, "never question an angel."

CHAPTER 7

At lunchtime, Rebecca munched on a tuna on rye from Charlie's Diner as she updated Bob via cell phone. "I'm telling you, Bob, this Carter character has Secret Santa written all over him. He's the patriarch of this town and—from what I've seen—the only one here in Mayberry with deep enough pockets. The only problem is, I can't seem to get in to see him."

"So, you're saying I should give away the Pacers tickets," Bob teased.

"Don't even think about it," Rebecca fired back.

"I've never let a little stumbling block get in my way. He's as good as mine."

"That's my girl," Bob said in his most patronizing tone. "And . . . before I forget . . . Ryan called."

Rebecca shifted her phone to the other ear. "Ryan? Really? What did he want?"

Bob smiled. He loved to bury the lead. "He wanted to know where you were."

"Tell me you didn't tell him," Rebecca said, nervously.

Bob hesitated for a moment to let the tension build. "Of course not. I told him you ran off with a Chippendale dancer named Lance."

Rebecca breathed a sigh of relief. "Good answer."

"Look, Chandler, I have a newspaper to run. Keep me in the loop."

"Will do," Rebecca said, clicking off her phone. She downed her last bite of sandwich and tossed the bag into a litter basket. "Okay, Mr. Carter. You've avoided me long enough."

Rebecca arrived back at the gate of the Carter mansion armed with new determination. She held down the buzzer an extra second, letting the invisible man on the other end know she meant business.

"May I help you?" the irritated voice finally answered.

"Rebecca Chandler, here for my three o'clock with Mr. Carter," she said firmly.

There was a pause followed by a condescending, "Are you certain?"

"Quite," Rebecca fired back, determined not to lose her momentum. "He said for me not to be late . . . and to be sure to let him know if I had any trouble getting in." Rebecca put her hand on the gate, poised to enter.

"That's odd," the voice said, after a moment of hesitation.

"Odd . . . how?" Rebecca shot back, no longer able to reign in her irritation.

"Well, Mr. Carter happens to be out of the country. Seems strange he would have made an appointment with you knowing he wasn't going to be in town."

Rebecca swallowed hard. It was think-on-your-feet-time. "Silly me. I must have written the appointment on the wrong day. When did you say you were expecting him back?"

"I didn't say," the voice replied, now thoroughly enjoying this little volley.

"Well, if you did say," Rebecca returned service, realizing that she was totally at his mercy, "the answer would have been . . ."

"Christmas Eve," the voice said smugly. "But, I don't believe he'll be seeing anyone. Good day."

Rebecca heard the now familiar sound of the intercom switching off. She stood still for a moment as his final words sank in. Of course. Secret Santa couldn't miss *Christmas Eve*. Now could he?

CHAPTER 8

lternator's shot."

Rebecca stood in front of a grease-stained Harley as he held the now defunct component in his hand.

"Well, can't you replace it?" Rebecca asked, hopefully.

"You mean, put in an 'alter-nate' alternator?" Harley grinned. Rebecca rolled her eyes, not in the mood for a stand-up routine. "Sure, but I gotta order it," he said, seriously.

"Okay, how long will that take?"

"Usually I can get an alternator in a few hours."

"Oh, good," Rebecca said, looking at her watch. "So, how about if I come back at five?"

"But . . . yours is a special order. It's gonna take a little longer."

Rebecca fixed her best business glare on him. "How long?"

Harley rubbed the grease from his hands with an even greasier rag and thought it over. "About three or four days."

Rebecca threw up her hands. "Harley, I have a deadline to meet."

Harley wiped his brow, smudging the grease all across his forehead. "I'll see what I can do . . . but, you know how things slow down around the holidays."

"Tell me about it."

It was only 5:30 but Charlie's Diner was already bustling with Hamden's "early-bird special" crowd. Rebecca commandeered a window booth where she worked on her laptop as she updated Bob by cellular.

"Everyone I've talked to points to Carter. He's this local Daddy Warbucks who likes to spread his green around. I'm surprised they haven't erected a statue of the old codger. Oh, by the way, I'm having dinner with the mayor. Should be good for a homespun quote or two."

Rebecca looked up as the front door opened, and Scotty wheeled in. She smiled at him, and he waved and headed over.

"Bob, gotta run. I'll check in later."

Rebecca watched Scotty make his way to her booth. He seemed to know everybody in the diner, and they all knew him, greeting him as he passed their tables.

"Hi, Scotty," Rebecca said.

"Hi, Miss Chandler. How's your story coming?"

"Fine . . . I think," she said. "And you can call me Rebecca." Scotty smiled as if he'd just been voted into some privileged adult inner circle. "So, Scotty," Rebecca said nonchalantly. "Have you ever met Mr. Carter?"

"Sure, lots of times," Scotty offered without hesitation.

"He seems like a very generous guy."

"Yeah. He's always doin' things for us . . . when he's in town."

"He's out of town a lot of the time, isn't he?" Rebecca said, like a lawyer leading a witness.

"He has to travel for his work," Scotty explained. "Callie and I do okay on our own though. She's been running the diner all by herself while Charlie's in Florida."

"Florida?" Rebecca said. "What's he doing there?"

"I think his father's kinda sick . . . ," Scotty said.

Callie whisked by their table loaded down with a tray of food. "Scotty, aren't you supposed to be doin' your homework?"

The boy sighed. His shoulders sagged. "I better get to work."

"Bye, Scotty." Rebecca watched him spin an about-face and roll off. At the sound of the front door opening, she looked up to see Winiford come flitting through, loaded down with shopping bags. She spotted Rebecca and made a beeline for her table. "Hi, Winiford," Rebecca said. "I'd ask you to join me but I have a meeting with the mayor." Rebecca glanced around the diner. "You haven't seen him, have you?"

"Every time I look in the mirror," Winiford replied, sliding into the booth seat.

"You mean you're the mayor?" Rebecca said, genuinely surprised.

"Going on six years," Winiford responded proudly. "I ran unopposed last election."

"Okay, then," a bemused Rebecca said, flipping open her notepad. "Mind if I ask you a few questions . . . Mayor?"

"Ask away, dear. I have nothing to hide. Except my special raspberry truffle recipe."

Rebecca looked Winiford in the eye. "What can you tell me about John Martin Carter?"

Winiford leaned forward and glanced around the diner as if the KGB might be listening in. "What would you like to know?"

"Well, for starters—just how rich is he?"

Winiford smiled. "Very rich. Old money rich."

Rebecca dug deeper. "And, it sounds as if he's not exactly stingy with his old money."

"He's the most charitable man in town," Winiford volunteered. "With the exception of Secret Santa, of course."

Rebecca sighed. She had grown weary of this game. "Come on, Winiford. Surely, it has occurred to you that Secret Santa and Carter are one and the same. I mean, he has motive, opportunity, and means. You don't have to be Sherlock Holmes to put two and two together."

Winiford took a sip of her water and cleared her throat. "Well, I don't know, dear. Hamden does have a population of nearly five thousand souls."

"Yes, but how many of those 'souls' can shell out four grand for a wheelchair?" Rebecca countered. "All I'm saying is: If I were a betting woman, I'd put my Secret Santa chips on John Martin Carter."

Winiford smiled sweetly, no longer willing to argue the point. "Well, I suppose you have your story then."

Rebecca closed her notepad. "Almost. Now, all I have to do is catch him in the act . . . Christmas Eve."

Winiford thought for a moment and then asked, "Say, what are you doing tonight?"

"I have no plans," Rebecca admitted.

"Perfect. Then, why don't you accompany me to the annual tree lighting. I think you might enjoy yourself."

Rebecca hesitated and then shrugged. "Sure, why not."

CHAPTER 9

As she wedged her way through the overflow crowd in the town square that night, Rebecca felt a twinge of melancholy. All around her were the happy signs of a small-town holiday. Couples held hands, people laughed, children played. It was like a great big family had gathered to ring in the Christmas season together.

Rebecca took it all in and came up feeling lonely. She wasn't sure what it was. Maybe it was the crispness in the night air, the smell of hot cider that drifted through the square, or the sight of the towering spruce but—

something about this town, these people, was different.

"No time for a pity party, Chandler," she thought to herself. "Just do your job and get out of town."

Rebecca spotted Callie and Scotty standing by the twenty-foot tree. The program was about to commence. She stepped up on a curb and bundled her coat snugly about her. For the moment, she was no longer a reporter covering a story. She was an eight-year-old girl again, shivering with anticipation.

Winiford stood on a small wooden platform, a microphone in her hand and her fur hat pulled down over her ears. "Ladies and gentlemen. May I have your attention, please." She held up her hand for quiet and scanned the crowd like a schoolteacher trying to pick out the disobedient children. "As mayor of Hamden," she continued, "I'd like to offer our heartfelt appreciation to the donor of this year's Christmas tree, our dear friend Mr. John Martin Carter."

Carter again, Rebecca thought, as the crowd erupted in applause. Winiford signaled Scotty to throw the switch. Suddenly, the perfectly shaped majestic tree was aglitter in shimmering white light. Caught up in the event, Rebecca gasped right along with the crowd. Maybe Harley was right about Hamden's spirit.

Through the crowd, Rebecca watched Scotty gaze in wide-eyed wonder at the glimmering tree. She could tell from the look on his face that the kid in the wheelchair still had unflinching faith in the magic of Christmas. She felt a sudden twinge of shame come over her. A lump rose up in her throat and she swallowed hard to stave off the tears. What right did she have to ever feel sorry for herself?

"Would you like a ride home, dear?" Winiford asked Rebecca. It was well after ten and only a few stragglers remained.

"No thanks. It's so beautiful out, I think I'll walk," she answered, gazing up at the starry winter sky.

Winiford smiled. "Suit yourself. I'll be off then. Good night."

"Good night," Rebecca said as she watched Winiford shuffle off toward her car, talking to herself and fishing in her purse for her keys.

On the walk back to Corapeake Cove, Rebecca took her time, trying to hold on just a little bit longer to the peaceful feeling the night had brought. She strolled past the gazebo where a young couple snuggled against the cold, oblivious to her presence. She crossed Main Street, past the darkened office of the *Hamden Herald* and by the shops now closed for the night. She paused outside the toy store and watched a Lionel train wind its way through a miniature village. She caught a quick glimpse of her reflection in the glass and couldn't help but notice the look of contentment on her face. What was it about this town? Were these people naïve . . . or did they know something she didn't?

Rebecca sighed heavily and started to cross the street. Suddenly, she stopped cold. A speeding SUV came barreling by, rolling through a muddy pothole and drenching her with cold, muddy muck from head to toe.

Rebecca gasped, collected herself, and surveyed the damage. Her shoes, her clothes, her face and even her hair were all coated with a brown slimy slush. Any flicker of affection she might have mustered for this cornpone town had just evaporated. "Hey!" she shrieked, her initial shock now giving way to indignation. The driver hesitated at the corner and began backing up. As he emerged from the car a moment later, he watched as his victim swiped the mud from her face. Her take-no-prisoners look stopped him cold in his tracks. Maybe he'd have been better off fleeing the scene.

"Merry Christmas to you too," Rebecca barked in a sarcastic rage.

"I'm sorry, I didn't see you," he said sincerely.

Rebecca felt her heart pounding. She was in no mood to accept an apology. "For not seeing me, your aim was perfect, buster."

Then, as he noticed the job he had done on her, the faint lines of an irrepressible grin began to creep up his face. He quickly snuffed it out. "I feel awful about this," he said. "Can I give you a ride somewhere?"

"A ride? A ride?" she stammered, finally addressing his question. "No, thank you. You've done enough already." Rebecca fought back tears of frustration. She didn't want to give him the satisfaction of seeing her meltdown. Despite the humiliation of the moment, she was determined to keep her composure. She tried to think peaceful thoughts, to remain calm. Then, without warning, her emotions erupted like Mount St. Helens.

"All I wanted was a nice, peaceful Christmas in Hawaii . . . I wanted to fall asleep on the beach smelling coconut oil and listening to waves crashing on the sand. I wanted to hear Don Ho, old and tired but still singing his Hawaiian heart out. And now look at me. I'm standing here covered with . . . muck . . . in a town that probably doesn't even have a decent dry cleaner!"

With that, she stalked off, leaving the driver bemused and bewildered.

CHAPTER 10

The mud had started to dry and crack by the time Rebecca shuffled through the door of the rest home. She checked herself in the foyer mirror and grimaced.

"My goodness. What happened to you?" Russell asked.

"Just some more of your small-town Christmas spirit."

Russell raised his eyebrows, but decided not to pursue the matter. Rebecca gave him one final defeated look and then slunk off down the corridor toward her room.

After a long, hot shower, she slipped into her pajamas and robe and headed for the kitchen. Rummaging around in the industrial refrigerator, she peeled the aluminum foil off a suspicious-looking container and struck gold. A half-eaten pumpkin pie was staring her in the face. She plopped the tin on the counter, grabbed a fork from the silverware drawer and dug in. Some women took bubble baths to relieve stress. Rebecca Chandler took calories.

"Comfort food?" Russell's deep voice broke her ravenous reverie. She was caught in the act.

"You mind?" she asked weakly.

"Not at all," he replied, "long as I can join you?"

"Be my guest," Rebecca shrugged.

Russell took a fork and plate from the cabinet and sidled up beside her. Rebecca cut him off a generous slice. "Much obliged," he said.

They ate in silence for a few minutes, each relishing the experience.

"This reminds me of when I was a kid," Rebecca said at last.

"Pumpkin pie, you mean?" Russell inquired.

"No. Sneaking down to the refrigerator in the middle of the night and pigging out."

Russell laughed. "I've sure spent my fair share of time in this refrigerator. I've got a sweet tooth that seems to kick in 'round midnight."

"Tell me about it," Rebecca said, shaking her head. "I find it impossible to sleep knowing that there are leftovers in my fridge. Especially dessert. And, there's nothing better for a woman's hips than cheesecake at two A.M." Rebecca shrugged and took another bite. "Russell, do you like working here?"

Russell pondered the question, his eyes squinting as if to help focus his thoughts. "Fact is," he said, finally, "I don't consider it work at all. I love what I do. I suppose most folks can't say that."

"But isn't it hard spending your whole life taking care of people?"

"Taking care of people makes me feel good," Russell replied. "Most of the people here—their families either live too far away or just don't have time for them anymore."

"That's sad," Rebecca said softly.

Russell nodded. "I guess, when you get right down to it, there's nothing worse than being alone."

Rebecca let his words sink in. He'd hit a nerve. She downed the last bite, got up from her stool and took the dishes to the sink. "You know . . . I think I'll turn in. It's been a long day."

"Good night, Rebecca," Russell said. He was starting to like this new visitor.

Rebecca closed her curtains, pulled down her covers, and reflected on her day. She was no closer to finding Secret Santa than the day she had arrived. That interview with the 104-year-old veteran was starting to look pretty good by comparison.

The not-so-subtle sound of someone clearing their throat interrupted her thought. Rebecca turned to find a white-haired lady propped up by a walker in her doorway.

"Oh, hello there. I hope I'm not disturbing you," the woman said. "I noticed your light was still on."

"Actually, I was just about to turn in," Rebecca said, hoping the old lady would get the hint.

No such luck. "My name's Miss Ruthie," the woman said, as she shuffled into the room.

"Pleased to meet you. I'm Rebecca."

Miss Ruthie sized up Rebecca as if it were the first

day of college, and she was her new roommate. "Russell tells me you're quite the bingo player," Rebecca said, filling the silence.

"And he tells me you're a reporter," Miss Ruthie countered.

"That's right. I am."

"Well, there's nothing shady going on around here if that's what you're after—unless you count Melvin Greenblatt cheating at cards. Corapeake Cove is a lovely place to live."

"Excuse me?" Rebecca said. She had no idea what the woman was talking about.

"I assume you're here to do some exposé on how old folks are so mistreated," Miss Ruthie explained. "I know what you people are like . . . always looking for dirt."

Rebecca smiled. If only Miss Ruthie knew. She'd kill for an elder abuse piece about now. "Not exactly. I'm actually in town on a Christmas story, and I'm just staying here because there was . . . no room at the inn, if you'll pardon the expression."

"Oh, well, that makes me feel much better," Miss Ruthie said, stopping suddenly as if some untoward thought had just come to mind. "You mean you're not spending the holidays with your family?"

Rebecca shook her head no, hoping Miss Ruthie would assume the subject was touchy and drop it. "Too bad," the old lady said sympathetically.

"You haven't met my family," Rebecca quipped.

"Maybe *you* just haven't learned to appreciate them," Miss Ruthie gently countered.

Rebecca smiled. "Maybe you're right. What about your family?"

Miss Ruthie smiled, patiently. "I have no family anymore." Rebecca suddenly felt like an insensitive jerk. "Unless you count the memories," Miss Ruthie continued.

This sobered Rebecca and she found herself fishing unsuccessfully for a suitable response as the old lady turned to go. "Good night, Miss Ruthie," she called out weakly.

Miss Ruthie turned back and smiled at her. "Good night, dear."

CHAPTER 11

Charlie's Diner was filled with the usual breakfast crowd the next morning. Sitting at her "regular booth," Rebecca had a cup of coffee and a bagel, along with the morning edition of the *Sentinel* spread out in front of her on the table. She glanced at the weather box at the top right corner of the front page. "Chance of snow for Christmas."

"See you later, Mr. Carter," Callie called out from behind the counter.

Carter? Rebecca dropped the newspaper and sprang from her seat like a jack-in-the-box. She grabbed an unsuspecting Callie by the arm. "Callie! Did you say Mr. Carter? *the* Mr. . . ."

Callie nodded as she gently extracted her arm from Rebecca's kung fu grip.

"But . . . he's not supposed to be back until Christmas Eve," Rebecca sputtered.

"Looks like he came home early," Callie said with a shrug. Rebecca dropped a five on the table and bolted for the door.

An instant later, she burst out of the diner and onto the sidewalk. She took a quick look in both directions. Nothing. The mysterious Mr. Carter had vanished into thin air.

Rebecca's near-miss Carter spotting filled her with renewed confidence. She headed directly for 391 South Madison. She dialed Bob on her cell phone as she peered through the iron bars of the mansion gate, determined to blow the lid off the Secret Santa mystery once and for all.

"Bob, I've got a lock on Secret Santa. And I'm moving in for the kill."

"I knew I could count on my ace reporter," he boasted. "I'm moving your story from features to the front page. We'll call it 'Secret Santa Revealed.' I'll tell the printer to double the run."

Rebecca smiled, mischievously. "But I do have one small request."

"Name it," Bob barked, propping his feet up on his desk.

"I want those Pacer tickets—now."

Bob sat up. "What? You're kidding?"

"Nope," Rebecca said. "I know you, and I want to make sure I have them in my hot little hands before you get my story."

"That's blackmail, Chandler."

"Here's the deal," Rebecca continued, ignoring his accusation. "If you want Secret Santa, then get me the tickets by tomorrow morning. Oh, and by the way—these terms are nonnegotiable. Have a nice day."

Rebecca flicked the off button and tucked her phone away. It was showtime. She stepped up to the buzzer, took a deep breath and . . . stopped. A thudlike noise came from just beyond the gate. She moved closer to the iron fence and peered through. She could see a man, partially obscured by the trees, stacking wood on the side of the house.

"Hey, you!" she called out. "Firewood guy."

The sound of wood chunks hitting the pile suddenly stopped, and the man looked around, trying to locate the source of the interruption.

"Over here," she shouted, "by the gate."

As the man brushed himself off and headed over, Rebecca plotted her strategy. Whoever he was, maybe he could help her get past the pesky voice on the intercom. If he was an employee of Carter's, he might be able to provide valuable information. Her hopes soared for a moment—but then her heart sank like a bowling ball in a swimming pool as the man stepped from behind the trees. "Oh, no. It's ... you," she said with a sudden rush of disappointment. There she stood—face-to-face with the mud-slinging SUV driver.

He smiled, recognizing her. "Afraid so. How are your clothes?"

"Probably ruined, thanks to you. You do know they have a class for people like you. It's called Driver's Ed."

"Thanks for the tip," he replied without missing a beat.

Rebecca was in no mood to be outwitted by Mr. J. Crew lumberjack. "The least you could do for ruining my favorite pair of shoes is to open this gate so I can keep my appointment."

"Your appointment?" he said with raised eyebrows.

"I am Mr. Carter's niece," Rebecca said, emphatically. "Grandniece, actually . . . and I guess he forgot I was coming today. You know how it is when you get to be . . . advanced in years. The memory is the first thing to go."

"So I've heard," he nodded sympathetically. "But, I'm afraid I can't let you in without Mr. Carter's permission."

Rebecca kept pushing. "Of course you can. All you have to do is open the gate and then you can go back to whatever it is you were doing. I'll be sure to put in a good word for you with my uncle."

"I didn't know Mr. Carter had a niece," he said quizzically.

Rebecca put her hands on her hips defiantly. "Well, maybe he doesn't choose to share all the details of his private life with . . . the firewood deliveryman. Did you ever think of that?"

The man smiled and shook his head as if he were thoroughly enjoying their little volley. "Well, to tell you the truth, Miss . . ."

"Chandler," Rebecca filled in sharply. "Rebecca Chandler."

"Miss Chandler, Mr. Carter usually takes a nap this time of day." Then, he winked and added. "You know how it is. At his age."

Rebecca glared a hole through him. This guy was really starting to get on her nerves.

"But," he added, "I do know for a fact that he's going to the mayor's Christmas party this evening." Then, he headed back to his wood stacking. Rebecca watched him for a moment and then turned and walked away. At least she had the information she needed to corner the old codger.

CHAPTER 12

By the time Rebecca strolled through the front gate of the Olde Hamden Inn, it was well after eight and the party had been going full throttle for the better part of an hour. She paused on the porch and looked through the window. The room was teeming with locals spruced up in green and red and sporting an assortment of Santa caps and big red rubber Rudolph noses. They were laughing and schmoozing and sipping cider amid decorations of wreaths, holly, and mistletoe. She spotted Callie and Scotty standing near the Christmas tree. George was at the piano plunking away, and

Winiford was beside him, belting out an off-key version of "Silver Bells." Harley stood nearby, decked out in red suspenders and a battery-operated, light-up tie that she suspected also played "Jingle Bells." She had to smile at the scene. Not even Norman Rockwell could have dreamed up such characters.

"Seasons greetings! How do you like my tie?" Harley asked as he ambushed Rebecca mere moments after she stepped through the door.

"Words fail me, Harley," she replied with a smile. "By the way, how's my car coming?"

"You got nuthin' to worry about, Miss Chandler. I'll have her up and runnin' in no time."

"Good. My feet hurt."

Rebecca slid past him and over toward Scotty.

"Hi, Scotty."

"Oh, hi Rebecca."

She pulled up a chair beside him, safely out of the crowd of partygoers. "This is some party," she said, looking around the room.

"So, did you find Secret Santa yet?"

Rebecca shrugged. "Not exactly."

"You think it's Mr. Carter, don't you?"

Rebecca nodded. "Let's just say he's my prime suspect."

"Why don't you just ask him?"

"Well, I'm having a little trouble tracking him down."

"Not anymore," Scotty said. "He just walked in."

Rebecca turned toward the front door, expecting to see a distinguished old man, perhaps with a top hat in one hand and a cane in the other. Instead, she saw a tuxedo, and inside, the most handsome man she had ever seen. She could hardly believe her eyes. It was the phantom SUV driver who'd drenched her with cold muck the night before, aka the firewood guy. Only now, the rugged lumberjack look had given way to a clean-shaven, modern-day Cary Grant who looked like he'd just stepped out of a limo at the Academy Awards. This was no old codger. This was take-your-breath-away handsome. She watched as Carter was immediately surrounded by friends: men slapping him on the back, women tiptoeing up to plant red lipstick marks on his cheeks.

So, this is John Martin Carter, she thought. Then she felt her cheeks flush as she remembered their conversation at the mansion that morning.

"Are you okay, Rebecca?" Scotty's small voice jolted her back to her senses.

"Uh, yeah. I'm fine. That's John Martin Carter?"

Scotty nodded his head up and down like a yo-yo.

"If you'll excuse me, Scotty, I have to go now." Rebecca began looking for an exit. Perhaps she could sneak out the French doors on the other side of the piano. They'd think she was just slipping out for a breath of fresh air and, instead, she would disappear into the night like D. B. Cooper.

"Hey there, Miss Chandler! There's somebody here who wants to meet you!"

Rebecca stopped in her tracks and turned toward the sound of Harley's bellicose voice. The garish mechanic was standing with his meaty arm around Carter's shoulder, his tie flashing like a strip club. The path to freedom was paved with quicksand. Rebecca was trapped. She could feel Carter's eyes on her, a smug look on his face as if he knew she was trying to make a break for it, and he was taking great enjoyment in foiling her attempt.

"If it isn't my favorite niece," he said. Her chagrin darkened another shade as he extended his hand. "John Martin Carter."

"I'm so embarrassed," Rebecca said.

"Don't be. Would you like me to . . . freshen up your cider?" Carter asked.

Rebecca looked him in the eyes and saw something there that wasn't half bad. "Sure."

From her perch on the piano bench, Winiford observed with interest the little scene playing itself out at the punch bowl. The handsome millionaire, the pretty reporter. She smiled and nudged George in the ribs, causing him to miss a note.

Rebecca fumbled to recover. "Unfortunately, we journalists . . . sometimes have to . . . how shall I put this . . . be 'creative' in order to get our stories."

"And I'm one of your stories?" Carter asked.

"Maybe."

"Well, here I am. I have nothing to hide."

Rebecca hesitated as if she couldn't remember what to do next. Then, she quickly regained her bearings, plucked her ever-present notebook from her purse and flicked her pen to the on position. "Okay. So what do you know about Secret Santa?" Rebecca watched his eyes, looking for any telltale sign that she'd hit a sensitive subject.

"About the same as everybody else," Carter responded nonchalantly. "In other words . . . not much."

"But, you're not just everybody else. Are you?" She suddenly felt like Perry Mason moving toward the witness box.

"You mean . . . you think *I'm* Secret Santa?"

Rebecca watched his body language. But Carter gave nothing away. He seemed to be enjoying their little verbal dance. "Yes, as a matter of fact, I do," she said, hoping to elicit a sudden confession and put the mystery to rest once and for all. Instead, he just chuckled and ladled himself another round of cider.

"How long have you been a reporter?" he asked.

"Almost ten years," she responded with a trace of defensiveness.

"Well, then I'm sure you've covered enough stories to realize the obvious answer isn't always the right one."

"Look," Rebecca said. "I've covered my fair share of . . . hard-hitting, um, news. And, I've learned plenty."

"Okay, then. I'll make you a deal: You have dinner with me tomorrow night and I'll give you an exclusive interview."

Rebecca hesitated, surprised by the offer. "You'll answer all my questions?"

"Within reason."

"Deal."

"Okay, how about seven o'clock. At my place."

"Your place?" Rebecca questioned.

Carter smiled. "Don't worry, it's strictly professional."

"Seven o'clock it is," she confirmed.

CHAPTER 13

The moment Rebecca arrived at Harley's Auto Shop the next morning, she had an uneasy feeling. He wasn't his usual goofy self. No jokes. No one-liners.

"Okay, where is it?" Rebecca asked.

Harley had a sheepish look on his grease-smudged face. "It's around back," he said glumly. Rebecca bolted out the door.

Behind Harley's Auto Shop was an assortment of rusted-out engine blocks, a few tires stacked next to an old axle, and a tarp covering what appeared to be a small car.

"What is going on here?" Rebecca asked.

"There was a little problem," Harley said reluctantly.

"Define *little.*"

"Well, I was testing out this new digital blowtorch the wife gave me for my birthday when there was a slight glitch in the starter switch."

"Bottom line me, Harley."

Harley took a deep, labored breath as if he were about to pass a kidney stone. Then he reached out, grabbed hold of a corner of the tarp and jerked it away with a sudden, swift motion.

Even Harley gasped at the sight. What Rebecca saw before her defied any sense of realistic expectation. Her precious vintage VW Beetle had been reduced to a smoldering hulk of charred metal. It looked as if a dozen Molotov cocktails had exploded inside it. Stunned, she struggled to speak.

"Oh, my—"

"Personally, I prefer the old torches," Harley added, scratching his scalp. "They're more predictable."

"My car . . ." Rebecca muttered. "You killed it."

"Oh, don't worry," Harley was quick to reassure. "I've got ya covered. My cousin Elden works over at Car World."

"Well, you better have a cousin that's a lawyer—because you're gonna need one!"

Rebecca drowned her sorrows with a bowl of chicken soup and a root beer float at Charlie's. She had expected a modicum of sympathy from Bob when she checked in by phone, but he burst out laughing instead, happily trumpeting the tale of her automotive misfortune to the entire newsroom.

"If you ask me, you shoulda set flame to that bucket of bolts years ago," he guffawed.

"Oh, fine idea, Bob," Rebecca replied sarcastically. "Now, what do you suggest I do for transportation?"

"I dunno. Get yourself something with a little style. Something from this century."

"With what you pay me? Please."

Bob chortled twice and switched gears. "How's the story coming? You beat a confession out of Secret Santa yet?"

"I'm having dinner with him tonight. And I'm wearing my brass knuckles."

"Maybe I underestimated you, Chandler," Bob grinned. "Maybe you *are* cut out for real news. So, what's the old buzzard like anyway?"

"Well, you know what they say; you've seen one old buzzard, you've seen them all."

Rebecca checked herself in the mirror. Would Carter realize that she'd bought a new dress for the occasion? Would that make her seem unprofessional? Flirtatious? Maybe she should wear glasses instead of contacts. That would send a message that she was there to do a story and nothing more. She glanced in the mirror and sighed. What a time for a bad hair day.

"My oh my! You look quite fetching." Rebecca turned to discover Miss Ruthie standing in her doorway. "What's the occasion?"

"Oh, nothing," Rebecca demurred. "Just a dinner."

Miss Ruthie raised her eyebrows. "It's for work, Miss Ruthie," Rebecca explained, "nothing exciting."

"Shame to waste a nice dress like that on a business dinner."

Rebecca began to formulate her dinner strategy on the walk to the mansion. She would stick to a game plan.

Keep bringing the subject back to Secret Santa. She was a reporter and no matter how charming he was, no matter how alluring the ambience, she would have his confession by the time she walked out the door. Secret Santa would be secret no more.

Rebecca pressed the intercom and the now solicitous voice came on immediately. "Miss Chandler, I presume."

Walking from the gate across the grounds to the front door, Rebecca's heart began to race. If she was just a newspaper reporter doing a job, why did she feel like a teenager going to her first prom?

Inside, the mansion was tastefully decorated in English country antiques with a few Georgio Leoni leather pieces thrown in for comfort's sake. A roaring fire crackled against the sound of classical music. Above the mantel in the library hung a painting of Hamden back when the town square was not much more than a post office, a drugstore, and a couple of shops. In the bookcase, there were novels, thick biographies, and a smattering of New Age self-help books. The walls were paneled, the artwork strictly American, and the oak floors covered with antique Persian rugs. It was masculine, but warm and inviting—like stepping into a Ralph Lauren ad.

Dinner was no less impressive. Halibut with caper sauce, asparagus, and arugula salad.

"That's some chef you have," Rebecca said, savoring every bite.

"Actually, I'm the chef."

"You expect me to believe *you* did all this?"

Carter smiled. "Cooking relaxes me."

"Let me guess, your grandmother is Julia Child."

"Not quite. My wife taught me to cook."

Rebecca stopped midbite and slowly put her fork down. "Your wife?"

"I married my college sweetheart—Emily. Cooking was one of her many talents."

"And will she be joining us?" Rebecca asked, trying to keep the edge out of her voice.

"Not likely. She passed away two years ago."

Rebecca swallowed hard. "I'm sorry, I didn't . . ."

Carter smiled reassuringly. "Don't apologize. You had no way of knowing. It's one of the reasons I travel so much. The only way I could deal with the loss was to throw myself headlong into my work."

"You must really miss her." Carter nodded and took another sip of wine. "So, speaking of your work: What is it you do that has you traipsing all over the world?"

"I spend a great deal of time in the rain forest."

"You're a tree hugger?"

"Not quite," he said patiently. "I'm there on behalf of the indigenous people. You see, there are tribes of natives living in the Amazon whose culture dates back thousands of years. Until recently, they've lived just as their ancestors did without interference. But now, big business is catching up to them, tearing apart their habitat. I'm an international lawyer and they are my clients. Last year, I filed a lawsuit on their behalf against three of the world's largest lumber companies."

"To make them stop harvesting there," Rebecca concluded.

Carter nodded. "Right. It's fulfilling work, but it keeps me out of town most of the time."

Rebecca was impressed. "But you made a point to be home . . . by Christmas Eve."

Carter smiled. "Well, you know what they say, there's no place like home for the holidays."

"And there's no particular reason you made sure you were here in time for Christmas?" she asked.

"Sure, there are lots of reasons," he answered.

"You know," Rebecca said, "if there were a contest for Mr. Ambiguity, you'd win first prize."

Carter smiled. "You want to know if I'm Secret Santa, don't you?"

"A simple yes or no would suffice."

"What if I were Secret Santa?"

"Then I'd be right. Because I think you are."

"What if I told you I didn't want to see that bit of news in your paper?"

Rebecca could feel her stomach tighten. Was he about to confess? "And, why may I ask, not?"

"Because Secret Santa couldn't exist in the public eye. It's his anonymity that allows him to do the most good for the most deserving people. And quietly serving others is what Secret Santa's all about."

"Which gives me all the more reason to suspect you," Rebecca said in her cross-examining voice.

Carter was unflappable. He smiled as if he found the whole discussion mildly amusing. "I'm flattered you think I'm that type of person."

Rebecca sat up straight, her radar on full alert, her mind racing with the possibilities. What was he about to tell her?

"But I'm afraid I'm going to have to disappoint you. I'm not Secret Santa."

Four simple words. "I'm not Secret Santa." He'd said

them as casually as if he were ordering a burger and fries.

"Really? You're not?"

Carter shook his head. "No, I'm not."

"Are you sure?"

"Yes," Carter laughed. "I'm sure."

"And, you're telling the truth?"

"The truth," he said. She could tell by the tone in his voice that he was serious.

They sat in silence as Rebecca tried to sort out the tornado of thoughts swirling around in her head. How could this be? He seemed like the perfect choice. He was caring, slightly mysterious, and loaded. And, more importantly, if Carter weren't Secret Santa . . . who was?

"I'm sorry to disappoint you," he said, breaking in on her mental storm.

"Disappointing me is hardly the problem."

"I hope this doesn't mean we can't see each other again," he continued.

"See . . . each other . . ." she stammered. "No. I mean . . . yes. Well, maybe . . . if my boss doesn't kill me first."

Rebecca was still sorting things out when Carter walked her to the front gate. She had arrived with a surefire plan to unmask the elusive Secret Santa and she was leaving with a career that was on life support.

"Sure I can't drive you back?" Carter asked.

"Thanks, but . . . I'd rather walk," Rebecca said, "I need some time to think."

"My loss," he said.

Rebecca started to walk away and then remembered her manners and turned back. "I had a really nice time."

"Me too," he said with a smile. Rebecca turned again to go. "Listen," he called after her. "I'm taking Scotty to pick out a Christmas tree tomorrow afternoon—if you'd like to join us."

Obsessed with her potential unemployment, Rebecca could only force a weak "maybe," as she started toward the gate.

Carter watched her walk off into a calm December night. But inside, Rebecca was feeling anything but calm.

CHAPTER 14

It's late, Chandler, whadaya want?" Bob belched into the phone. Before calling her bombastic editor with the bad news, Rebecca had donned her pajamas and curled up on the bed with a box of chocolates. By the time she'd mustered the courage to dial his number, the box was nearly empty and little white wrappers were littered all around her. Bob was just about to leave the office for the night and was in an especially foul mood. So Rebecca decided to skip the idle chitchat and cut to the chase.

The good thing about Bob was he never let her

down. As soon as she dropped the bomb, he exploded.

"Bob, calm down—"

"Don't tell me to calm down!" Bob shrieked. Rebecca could imagine him pacing around like a caged bull, steam spewing out of both ears. "You told me you had Secret Santa in the bag! I've been promoting this stupid story everywhere. On the radio, local TV . . . I even hired one of those little planes to drag a banner all over town. And now the day before the deadline you call me up and tell me . . . Secret Santa is . . . still . . . still . . . a secret!"

Rebecca sighed. It was impossible to reason with him when he was like this. "I made a little mistake," she said finally.

"Little?!"

"All right, a huge mistake . . . but I'll make it up to you. I promise."

"I don't want you to make it up to me! I want you to find my Secret Santa, and you've got forty-eight hours to do it!"

"Bob, I—" Rebecca stopped. He'd already hung up. Rebecca dropped the phone on the bed and looked back at the half-eaten box of chocolates in front of her. Why not? She plucked out another piece and took a comforting bite.

"Forty-eight hours," she said aloud. "Two days. It's impossible . . . there's no way . . ."

Rebecca turned to discover Miss Ruthie listening from the doorway. "Go right ahead, dear. I certainly don't want to interrupt."

"Oh, hi there, Miss Ruthie," Rebecca stammered. "I was just—"

"No need to explain," Miss Ruthie said, as she entered the room. "As a matter of fact, most of the residents here at Corapeake Cove talk to themselves from time to time."

Rebecca smiled sheepishly. "Sorry, it's just that I promised my editor this story and it's not going so well."

Miss Ruthie brightened. "Oh. What seems to be the trouble? Maybe I can help."

Rebecca shifted on the bed and looked up at Miss Ruthie, prepared to reject her kind offer and then it dawned on her—maybe she really could help. "Well, I came to Hamden to do a story on Secret Santa, to try to find out who he is."

"Secret Santa?" Miss Ruthie said thoughtfully. "I see."

"I was so sure it was Carter."

"Carter?" the old lady interjected. "You mean John Martin Carter?"

"One and the same."

A smile came to Miss Ruthie's face. "Sweet boy. I was his fourth-grade teacher. Always turned in his assignments on time. But he's far too busy to be Secret Santa."

"Yeah, well, it would have made my life a whole lot simpler if he were. Now I don't have a story and my boss is about to send me back to obituaries."

"You know, I've been around this town a long time and if you ask me, Secret Santa's never been that much of a mystery."

Rebecca suddenly perked up. "What do you mean?"

"Well, I've always suspected it was the Bonneville sisters."

"The who?"

"They're spinsters. A touch eccentric, but very well-off. And they have lots of time on their hands. They live in a big house on Elm Street. If I were you, I'd check them out."

Rebecca wrinkled her brow. Miss Ruthie's revelation may have just put her back in the game. "The Bonneville sisters, huh?"

CHAPTER 15

Rebecca was up early the next morning and found Russell reading the paper at his station in the rest home foyer. "Morning, Russell. I need to borrow the phone book. I've finally got a hot lead on Secret Santa."

Russell reached beneath the desk, retrieved the Hamden White Pages and handed it to her. "Secret Santa?"

Rebecca explained as she hurriedly flipped to the Bs. "I thought it was Carter, but he was a wild-goose chase and now I think I'm back in business. There they are.

Betty and Beatrice Bonneville. 21 Elm Street." Rebecca hurriedly scribbled down the address and phone number on her notepad and then handed the book back to Russell. "Thanks. Gotta run."

"Oh, Rebecca. I almost forgot. Winiford called. Seems a room's opened up at the inn. She's holding it for you."

Rebecca paused in the doorway and stared at him. At last, her ticket out of this dreary place. She looked around, noticed the photos on the wall in the entry hallway. They commemorated ninetieth birthday parties, sing-alongs, bingothons, and quiet evenings in front of the television. To the right was another section of pictures, "In Memory of Our Friends." The quick survey across the montage stopped her. She already knew most of the residents by name. She sighed and turned back to Russell. "Would you do me a favor, Russell. Tell Winiford . . . I think I'll stay here at Corapeake Cove." Russell smiled and nodded as Rebecca headed out the door.

Betty Bonneville answered the phone on the first ring, and Rebecca set up an appointment for that afternoon. She grabbed a quick muffin and coffee at Charlie's and then headed over to the Hamden library where she did a little background research on the sisters. They were locals, born and raised. Rebecca could imagine them scheming, weaving their little Secret Santa web, scouring the local paper for stories of the needy and downtrodden. This time she was sure she had her pigeons. And in just a few hours, she'd have her story. Feeling secure, she decided to go meet Carter and Scotty.

When Rebecca arrived at the Christmas tree lot, she immediately spotted Carter and Scotty cruising the rows, critically studying each spruce and pine. She stopped for a moment and watched them. Scotty seemed to be in heaven, chattering excitedly about the various prospects while Carter was the picture of patience, readily analyzing each tree. Rebecca's cell phone rang; she checked the caller ID and clicked on. "Bob, you're never going to believe it. We've been looking for Secret Santa when, in actuality, we should have been looking for Secret San*tas*," she said, emphasizing the plural. "And on top of that, we had the sex wrong but that's neither here nor there."

She paused to let Bob get a word in.

"Okay, I will tell you what I'm babbling about . . . Secret Santa is two old biddies, sisters who never married. They have lots of time to kill between fine-tuning their strudel recipes and knitting sweaters for their pet poodles. Oh, by the way, I'm seeing them later this afternoon. In other words, I should have this story wrapped up with time to spare."

Then, Scotty yelled out, "Rebecca, come look! John said I could get an eight-footer if I want! And there's this really cool one over here with a top that's perfect for a star!"

Rebecca pulled the phone away from her ear for a moment. "Wow, that's great, Scotty." And then back to business. "Look, Bob. Gotta go. I'll update you later." Rebecca shut her phone and slipped it back into her pocket.

"Sounds like you're busy," Carter observed. "It was nice of you to give up your afternoon."

"Well, it *was* Lawrence Welk day at the home—but you can't have everything."

The sound of a car honking interrupted the conversation. They all three turned toward the parking lot just in time to see a silver 700 Series BMW come to an abrupt halt, making a skid mark in the gravel. Rebecca did a double take. The vanity plate was all too familiar. "RYNS BMR."

Rebecca felt a knot in her stomach. What on earth was Ryan doing here? Before she could wrap her mind around that question, he had climbed out of his car and was heading toward her like a little boy who'd just found his lost puppy.

"Becka," he yelled to her.

Rebecca glanced at Carter and Scotty. They were both looking at her, waiting for an explanation.

"It's complicated," was all she managed to get out before Ryan swept her up in a jubilant embrace. "Ryan, what are you—?"

"Oh, baby. How I have missed you," he said as she struggled to break free from his death grip.

"But, how did you—?"

"Your insurance adjuster told me you were here . . . in Hampton."

"Hamden."

"Whatever."

"And what are you doing talking to my insurance adjuster?"

"We sauna together. Sorry to hear about your car." Ryan stepped back and looked her up and down. "You look wonderful. Seeing you is like waking up from an endless nightmare." Ryan glanced over at Carter and Scotty as though they were unwanted eavesdroppers. "Ryan Corbin," he said abruptly, thrusting out his hand to Carter. "Rebecca's significant other."

"Ex significant other," Rebecca corrected, but Ryan didn't seem to hear her. He had already moved on to Scotty.

"Hello there, young fella. How are you today?"

Scotty stiffened. "Fine," he said politely.

Rebecca turned to Carter. "Can you give us a minute?"

Carter nodded and tightened his hands on the wheelchair grips. "Come on, Scotty. I hear they keep the really good trees out back. Let's go check it out."

Rebecca watched them until they moved out of earshot. Then she turned and fired at Ryan. "Ryan, what is going on here? I thought you were off mating souls with . . . Nina?"

Ryan dropped his head. "Nina wasn't her real name."

Rebecca raised her eyebrows. "Oh."

"It was either Dolores or Abigail, depending on which alias you believe. I woke up one morning and she was gone. So was my wallet, my Rolex, and my handcrafted Italian shoes. She cleaned me out, Becka. And according to the police, she's run the same scam on several other unsuspecting businessmen. Can you believe it?"

Rebecca crossed her arms defiantly. "Call *Dateline*. Maybe they'll do a story. And ask them to keep your face in shadow so the whole world won't see what an idiot looks like."

Undeterred, Ryan plowed ahead. "Becka, I don't know how I could have been so stupid. I had the most wonderful, caring woman in the world and I just . . . threw it all away." Ryan wiped his eye with the back of his hand, working up a tear. "Now, all I can do is hope that . . . somehow, some way . . . you'll find it in your heart to forgive me."

Ryan choked up as if the emotion of the moment made it impossible to utter even one more syllable. There was a time when such a display might have garnered her sympathy. That time had long since passed.

"Ryan, you can't just come waltzing back into my life like this."

"Why not?"

"Well, for one thing, I happen to be working on a story. And, secondly . . . I've kind of moved on."

"It's that guy, isn't it? I'm surprised at you, Rebecca. I thought you had more journalistic integrity than to get involved with the subject of one of your stories."

"That 'guy' has nothing to do with it. This has everything to do with you, Ryan. You betrayed me, dropped me like a bad habit. And now that things didn't quite work out the way you planned, you come crawling back, expecting me to just forget 'Nina' ever happened."

Ryan swallowed hard, kicking into victim-mode. "Becka . . . I've been through . . . a great deal these last few days. And you have to believe me when I tell you, I need you in my life. What can I do to make things right? Just tell me and I'll do it."

Rebecca looked him in the eye. "Okay, I'll tell you." Ryan perked up. "You can walk over to that fancy car of yours, get behind the wheel, and drive out of town. When you reach the town limits, keep going. And, in the future, if you ever have the urge to contact me in any way, shape, or fashion, resist it with all your might."

Ryan looked perplexed. "What are you saying?"

"Let me bottom line it for you, Ryan. It's over." With that, Rebecca gave him one last glare of defiance, then turned and walked away.

Carter returned just in time to overhear the grand finale. Embarrassed, Rebecca decided not to explain. "Well," she said finally, "did you guys find a tree?"

CHAPTER 16

With Scotty's tree tied to the roof of the SUV, Carter drove Rebecca to the Bonneville home. She waved as the two of them drove away, heading off to transform the plain Scotch pine into a concoction of shiny balls, tinsel, and multicolored lights. As they disappeared down the street, she found herself wishing she were going with them. But duty called. She had less than forty-eight hours to get her story. Fortunately, it was looking like Miss Ruthie had saved her from Bob's wrath.

The mailbox read Bonneville. The white picket fence

surrounding the neat little front yard looked like it had been painted fresh that morning. Hanging by the door was a little swaying sign that read: Welcome to Our Humble Home. Rebecca was sure she had found her elusive quarry.

Rebecca raised her hand to knock but before she could make the first rap, the door opened. There they stood, two pleasant, pear-shaped, white-haired ladies. It was as if she had interrupted them on their way to an audition for *Arsenic and Old Lace*. As they invited her inside, Rebecca inhaled a deep whiff of mothballs.

The sisters led her to the parlor where they offered her their famous sugar cookies and a cup of tea.

"You know, I've never cared for mint tea," Betty complained.

"But it's good for the digestion and you know you have a delicate stomach," Beatrice countered.

"Good for the digestion? Tea? Why, that's absurd."

Rebecca cleared her throat. "Excuse me, but could we possibly get started?"

The sisters looked at her with puzzled powdered faces. "Started with what, dear?" Betty asked.

"With my interview. That's the reason I'm here. Remember?"

"Oh, yes," Beatrice said. "Remember, Betty, she wants to talk to us about a story."

"Of course," Betty said, putting her tea aside. "Go right ahead."

Rebecca dove in. "Thank you. Okay, let's get right to the point. What do you ladies know about Secret Santa?"

The sisters looked at each other, eyebrows raised. When they turned back to Rebecca they had almost identical quizzical looks on their faces. "Why, not a thing, dear," Betty responded sweetly.

"We are blissfully ignorant of the whole affair," Beatrice added.

Rebecca sighed, no longer in the mood for coy evasion. "What if I told you I think you two are Secret Santa?"

The Bonnevilles looked at each other again and then began to giggle, making dainty little chirps that turned to chuckles, then to gales of squealing laughter.

"What's so funny?" Rebecca asked.

"Why, we couldn't possibly be Secret Santa, dear," Betty replied, struggling to bring her tittering under control.

"And why not?"

"Because," Beatrice said, leaning confidentially toward Rebecca, "we're . . . Jewish."

Rebecca glared incredulously at the two sisters. As she walked back to the rest home, the words "unemployment line" danced like sugar plums in her head.

"Why didn't you tell me they were Jewish?" Rebecca asked as she cornered Miss Ruthie. Undeterred, Miss Ruthie continued her game of solitaire.

"Who dear?" Miss Ruthie finally replied as if she had no idea what Rebecca was talking about.

"The Bonneville sisters."

The retired schoolteacher tilted her head to the side, a giant question mark on her face. "They are? Oh, my. I had no idea."

"I'm finished," Rebecca sighed, slumping into a chair. "I came here to find Secret Santa and all I've come up with is a big, fat zero. And I'm supposed to be an investigative reporter. Yeah, right."

Miss Ruthie smiled and played her next card. "Now, now, nothing's ever quite as bad as it seems. My father used to say: 'It's always darkest just before the dawn.'"

"Not in my experience," Rebecca lamented, her body language screaming defeat. "Sometimes it just keeps getting darker until you can't see anything."

Miss Ruthie put down her cards and sighed pensively. This called for an intervention of good old-fashioned wisdom. "Do you remember when it was you stopped believing in Santa Claus?"

"I know exactly," Rebecca replied without a moment's

hesitation. "I was in second grade. My parents wanted to take a family trip to Florida for Christmas, and I pitched a major league fit because I was afraid Santa wouldn't know where to find me. My parents tried everything but nothing could appease me. My dad was getting more and more irritated with my whining and then he just burst out with it: 'Only babies believe in Santa Claus.'" Rebecca stopped. Recalling the memory had sobered her. She was surprised by how much it still hurt. Six little words with such a big impact. She felt silly that she could still feel the effects all these years later.

"Well, maybe it's time you started believing again," Miss Ruthie said kindly.

Rebecca smiled. Talking to Miss Ruthie was comforting, like a trip to Grandma's. Rebecca curled up in the chair and started to bare her soul: Her job. Her sister. Ryan. Woe after woe.

Hours passed before Rebecca noticed the glazed look on Miss Ruthie's face.

"I didn't mean to take up your whole evening, I'm so sorry."

"It's okay, dear. But would you mind . . . reading to me before you go? It helps me fall asleep."

Rebecca hesitated for a moment and then nodded. "Sure. What would you like?"

Miss Ruthie pointed toward her nightstand. "That book there. The one with the tattered cover."

Rebecca spotted a well-read volume on the bedside stand next to the box of tissues. She picked it up and examined it, running her fingers across the aged leather cover. *"The Gift of the Magi,* by O. Henry," she read softly.

"It was a Christmas present from my father when I was a very young girl," Miss Ruthie explained.

Rebecca pulled her chair up next to Miss Ruthie's bed and carefully opened the book to the first page, to a drawing of a poorly furnished room. She cleared her throat and began to read. "One dollar and eighty-seven cents. That was all. And sixty cents of it was in pennies. Pennies saved one and two at a time. Three times Della counted it. One dollar and eighty-seven cents. And the next day would be Christmas." Rebecca paused and glanced at Miss Ruthie. The old lady's eyes brightened as if hearing Rebecca read was sending a charge of light through her. Rebecca continued. Just outside the door, Russell paused on his evening rounds to eavesdrop. He had the look of a man well-pleased. Rebecca read until Miss Ruthie fell asleep. Then she pulled the blanket up over her new friend and tiptoed out of the room.

CHAPTER 17

When Rebecca awoke the next morning, she sat bolt upright in bed. She had exactly twenty-four hours to find Secret Santa and the suspect fountain was all dried up.

After a shower and a quick "good morning" to Miss Ruthie, she headed to the diner with a hunger for a Charlie's Special #2, eggs over medium, extra bacon, and a big hunk of butter for her rye toast.

As she crossed the town square, she noticed a small cluster of locals gathered outside the diner door. Winiford, George, and Harley were among them. She wondered if maybe Callie was running late. But then Rebecca spotted her in the crowd—she was hanging a "Closed" sign on the door.

"Callie, what's going on?" Rebecca asked, stepping through the throng of locals. Then she noticed Callie's face. She'd been crying. A twinge of fear suddenly gripped Rebecca. "Is Scotty okay?"

"He's fine," Callie nodded, her lower lip quivering. "Charlie's not coming back."

Rebecca looked around at the solemn faces—they were all staring at Callie. "Why not?"

"His dad died," George chimed in. "He's staying in Florida . . . to take care of his mother."

"Charlie's is no more. He's already sold the place," Winiford said, putting her arms around Callie's shoulders to comfort her.

"To whom?" Rebecca asked, looking around at the assembly. She was met with blank stares. Nobody knew.

"I bet some city folks bought it," Harley theorized. "Probably put in one of those organic juice bars."

Rebecca glanced back at Callie. She could read the heartbreak in the girl's face and she felt for her. "What are you going to do?"

Callie bit her lip, trying to squeeze back the tears.

"Look for a job, I guess. I gotta figure out a way to take care of me and Scotty." Then the emotional dam broke and the tears started streaming down her cheeks. She turned and worked her way through the crowd, walking quickly down the sidewalk toward home.

Rebecca and the others watched her go. When she'd rounded the corner out of sight, George sighed heavily. "I guess there's some things that just aren't meant to last forever. Come on—let's don't forget we've got the pageant tonight. And you know what they say: The show must go on."

George's words dispersed the gathering until only Winiford and Rebecca remained. "Just so you know," the innkeeper began, "you're always welcome in Hamden, Rebecca Chandler." Winiford turned to walk away, then remembered something. "I almost forgot." She retrieved a gold key from her pocket and placed it in Rebecca's palm. "It's a key to the city. It's only symbolic, of course . . . but the sentiment is genuine."

Rebecca looked into Winiford's eyes. For once in her life, she felt speechless. Winiford smiled and then turned to cross the street, waving and calling out to passersby as if she owned the town. What was it about this place— this place that felt like a Frank Capra movie.

Rebecca made good use of her last day in Hamden. She spent it holed up in the library, surfing the web for "reporter wanted" ads. She tried to feel sorry for herself but then would remember Callie's predicament and feel guilty for her self-pity. From her perch by the library window, she had a panoramic view of the town square as it busied itself for the evening's event. The Hamden Christmas Pageant was renowned throughout Indiana, and the tourists were already arriving in their campers, pickup trucks, suburbans, and station wagons. The Olde Hamden Inn would be full again and the streets would be teeming with tourists, looking for a quick taste of a small-town American Christmas. The next morning the pageant would be nothing but a memory and the visitors would all be off again, rolling out of town as quickly as they'd arrived. They'd line up at Harley's Auto Shop to fill up, and he'd send them on their way with a corny joke and a wave of his chubby hand. Suddenly, Rebecca felt a lump in her throat as the realization dawned on her: She would be leaving too.

By the time Rebecca arrived in the town square that evening, hundreds of people had already gathered for the pageant. She looked at the shimmering star at the top of the Christmas tree, then to the clear sky above. Maybe that white Christmas rumor would turn out to be just that.

"There you are," a familiar voice called out. Moments later, Carter was standing beside her holding two cups of steaming hot chocolate. "I've been carrying this around hoping I'd find you here."

He handed Rebecca a cup and she took a sip. "Thanks. So, you're not participating in the pageant?"

Carter shook his head. "I prefer the shadows to the spotlight." Rebecca caught a glint in his eyes and her heart jumped. Could he be Secret Santa after all? Could he have lied to protect his precious anonymity, and now he was feeling guilty about it?

Rebecca's eyes lingered on him for a moment and then a shrill blast from a French horn turned her attention to the footlights just as Winiford, dressed in a long white robe, stepped from the wings to take center stage. There, she waited patiently for the murmuring crowd to quiet so she could begin.

"And lo, the angel of the Lord came upon them, and

the glory of the Lord shone 'round about them; and they were sore afraid." With that, Scotty rolled onstage, dressed as an angel. Two rather large, feathery, white wings were attached to the back of his chair, and Rebecca couldn't help but chuckle. She glanced at Carter. He was equally amused. Scotty had kept his role a well-guarded secret. He had wanted to surprise Carter. And he did.

An hour later, another Hamden Christmas Pageant had passed into history. And Rebecca and Carter chaperoned Callie and the angelic Scotty home.

"Nice job tonight, champ," Carter complimented. "You look good in wings."

"Yeah, Scotty," Rebecca added. "You're the first angel I've ever seen—" She caught herself.

"In a wheelchair?" Scotty finished with a grin. "There's all kinds of angels, you know."

Rebecca looked over at Callie. The young waitress couldn't be worried—not tonight. She was too proud.

"Oh, I almost forgot," Rebecca said, reaching into her coat pocket. She stepped over to Scotty and handed him a small white envelope. "Merry Christmas."

The boy looked at Carter for an explanation but got only a "your-guess-is-as-good-as-mine" shrug. Scotty tore open the envelope and out fell two small pieces of paper. Scotty's face lit up like the Fourth of July. "Wow! Pacers tickets . . . courtside. This is awesome!"

Then, before Rebecca knew what hit her, Scotty wheeled over and locked her waist in a big bear hug. She was momentarily thrown off by the gesture and then she did what seemed the most natural thing in the world. She leaned down and hugged him back. And when it came time to let go, she decided to hold on just a little bit longer.

CHAPTER 18

The walk back to the rest home reminded Rebecca a little of *It's a Wonderful Life:* Jimmy Stewart and Donna Reed strolling through the quiet neighborhood, stopping to throw a rock at the old Granville place. The difference being, Carter wasn't singing "Buffalo Gals" and they hadn't just danced into a swimming pool. The walk was only five blocks, but in that short distance Rebecca had come to the conclusion that she liked this guy, this John Martin Carter.

"So this is it, I guess," Carter said pensively. "Tomorrow you go home."

Rebecca nodded. "And without Secret Santa. Unless you want to cop a last minute plea to save a poor reporter's job."

She knew that if Carter really was the mysterious philanthropist, now was the perfect time for him to give her some kind of sign. All she'd need was a wink, a glance, a furtive little double entendre.

"I'm afraid I can't help you," he said.

When they arrived back at the rest home, there was an awkward pause by the front door that reminded Rebecca of a first date.

"So, was your stay in Hamden as terrible as you thought it would be?" he asked.

"Oh, it had its moments," she said with a flirty smile.

And then he took a deep breath, the kind a man takes when he's about to say something of major importance. Rebecca braced herself. This could be it. An eleventh-hour confession. "You know I'm a pretty good Parcheesi player—if you'd like to invite me in," Carter said with a twinkle.

Rebecca tried to hide her disappointment. "Sorry, I'm not allowed visitors after eight," she said. "They've probably run out of prune whip by now anyway."

"Too bad." Carter laughed.

Rebecca wondered what was going on in the mind behind that handsome face. Was he interested in her?

"I wish . . . we could have spent more time together," he said.

"Yeah, well I was far too busy ruining my career," Rebecca lamented. Carter smiled, knowing she was only half kidding.

"So, I guess you'll be heading back to the rain forest," she probed.

"As soon as the holidays are over. But I hope our paths will cross again."

"Well, if you're ever in Indy . . . I'm in the book," she said.

With that, Rebecca spontaneously leaned in and planted a kiss on his cheek. Then, as if on cue, she turned and fled like a schoolgirl at a fire drill.

The next morning as she packed to go home, Rebecca had a sinking feeling in her stomach, and it had nothing to do with her impending unemployment—or the prune juice, for that matter. Hamden, it seemed, had cast its spell. She had actually grown attached to the little town tucked away among the Indiana cornfields.

She took one last look around the room for stray belongings, then zipped her bag, just as Miss Ruthie appeared in the doorway.

"I suppose you were planning on leaving without saying good-bye," she accused.

"Not a chance," Rebecca replied.

"Good. Because I have something for you." With that, Miss Ruthie disappeared down the hall. Rebecca checked her watch. The cab would be there any minute. Miss Ruthie returned moments later holding a small, thin package wrapped in plain brown paper. She handed it to Rebecca. "Merry Christmas."

Rebecca felt surprisingly self-conscious. "Miss Ruthie . . . you shouldn't have." She peeled away the paper to reveal the familiar old worn book, the one she'd read to Miss Ruthie to help her get to sleep. Rebecca swallowed the lump in her throat and blinked back a tear. *"The Gift of the Magi.* But . . . your father gave you this."

"And now I'm passing it on to you." Miss Ruthie smiled. "Such is the nature of giving."

Rebecca was touched, as if someone had just jabbed a hypodermic needle filled with the Christmas spirit into her backside. As she looked up, she noticed the smile of satisfaction covering Miss Ruthie's wrinkled face.

"I do have one request, however," Miss Ruthie asked.

"Anything." Rebecca complied.

"I'd like to hear you read the ending, just one more time."

Rebecca looked down at the leather-bound edition in her hand and, with a deep breath, slowly opened it to the last page. When she began to read she was surprised by the sound of her own voice. She was reading with a feeling, a passion she hadn't felt in a long time. "And here I have lamely related to you the uneventful chronicle of two foolish children in a flat who most unwisely sacrificed for each other the greatest treasures of their house. But in a last word to the wise of these days let it be said that of all who give gifts these two were the wisest. Everywhere they are wisest. They are the Magi."

Rebecca sat perfectly still, the meaning of the words resonating in her, the sweetness of the moment filling her with a feeling of peace. *So, this is what the Christmas spirit feels like,* she thought.

"O. Henry had something to teach us all," Miss Ruthie said softly.

"I feel bad," Rebecca said. "I don't have a gift for you."

Miss Ruthie reached over and took Rebecca's hand. "Oh, but you do."

"I do?"

Miss Ruthie nodded. "I've already been the lucky recipient. You give of yourself. Remember the lesson of the Magi, Rebecca. The most important gifts are from the heart."

Rebecca pondered the words of wisdom as Miss Ruthie walked to the door, then stopped and turned back. "Russell will want to say good-bye, you know."

"I'll see him on the way out," Rebecca replied.

"I don't think so. He's not in today."

Rebecca arched her eyebrows. "Not in? I thought he lived here."

Miss Ruthie looked surprised. "Live here? I suppose it does seem that way, doesn't it?" She paused and then added, "I know he'll be sorry to have missed you. Merry Christmas, dear," she added with a twinkle. "And do stay in touch."

Rebecca watched as Miss Ruthie crossed the hallway, entered her room and closed the door. Outside, a car horn tooted twice. Her taxi had arrived.

Rebecca headed for the front door, then stopped. She went to the desk and grabbed the Hamden phone book before going outside.

The driver loaded Rebecca's suitcase into the trunk. It was a cold morning and, instinctively, she checked the sky. Not a cloud in sight. No white Christmas this year for Hamden.

"Is that everything, ma'am?"

Rebecca was silent, staring at the building as if saying good-bye to a treasured friend. "Forget something?" the driver prodded.

"No," Rebecca answered finally. "I didn't forget anything."

As the cab rolled out past the Corapeake Cove sign, Rebecca savored the memories of her stay in Hamden. Miss Ruthie. Pumpkin pie with Russell. Dinner with Carter. Mayor Winiford. Scotty in his angel wings. A waitress named Callie. George, the crusty old newspaperman. She vowed to remember them all—even Harley.

CHAPTER 19

Driving through the quiet Main Street, Rebecca took it all in one last time. To the casual observer it might seem that Hamden, Indiana, was nothing more than a smudge on the road map, a rest stop on the way to more exciting destinations. Rebecca knew better. Hamden was special. She couldn't quite put her finger on it, but one thing she knew for sure—she was leaving this town a better person than when she'd arrived.

She glanced up just in time to read a street sign outside her window. "Maplewood Drive. Turn right here, please," she told the driver.

A few minutes later, the cab stopped in front of a single-story shanty with a leaning front porch and a tiny, neatly trimmed front yard.

From her seat in the back of the taxi, Rebecca pondered her options. Maybe she should just keep on going. After all, the place looked empty. Maybe he had relatives and was spending the day with them. She checked her watch. The meter was running. Finally, she reached for the handle and opened the door. "I'll be right back," she said.

The porch creaked as she stepped cautiously up to the front door. Rebecca felt awkward and out of place—like a reluctant trick-or-treater. She reached out and rapped on the door lightly—then, when there was no answer, again, this time more forcefully. Nothing. Finally, she stepped over to the window and peered inside. The living room was modest. A small Christmas tree stood by the fireplace, and a few Christmas cards were lined up on the mantel.

Then she heard a noise, a high-pitched whining. It stopped, and then a second later, started again. Rebecca stepped back from the window and listened. Again, a stop and start. Then, once more. She decided to follow the sound.

Rounding the corner of the house, Rebecca saw an old elm tree with big, sprawling branches, the type that would cast plenty of welcome shade on hot summer days. She saw an old rusty tractor that looked as if it hadn't been ridden in twenty years, a well-stocked bird feeder, and an old shed tucked far back at the edge of the property. The sound of a table saw whined again, and Rebecca could now tell it was coming from inside the shed.

She approached the wooden shack and peered through a dusty window, but all she could make out was the dim glow of a swinging bulb and the shadow of someone moving around inside.

Steeling her nerves, she slowly pushed open the rickety wooden door.

When she stepped inside she was met by the pleasantly sweet smell of sawdust, and it put her immediately at ease. Her eyes widened in girlish wonder. She looked around, drinking it all in. It was just as she had always imagined Santa's workshop would be. Spread out across the workbench were gifts in various stages of completion. Rebecca was transplanted to another time and place, when as a little girl she whispered into the ear of some minimum-wage department store Santa, believing with all her might he alone held the key to her heart's desire. It was the peace she'd felt hearing her grandfather read "The Night Before Christmas" by the fireplace on Christmas Eve. It was that feeling of anticipation and mystery when she'd wake up Christmas morning, slip out of her bed before anyone else was awake, and sneak downstairs to discover the red-, green-, and gold-wrapped bounty spread out beneath the tree. Rebecca couldn't begin to explain it in a million years, but, somehow, this tiny shed managed to capture the magic of Christmas. And yet, she knew that it wasn't just the room that made her feel that way. It was the man leaning over the bench, goggles protecting his eyes from the specks of wood that flew up from the two-by-four he was sawing. When Rebecca stepped forward, he spotted her out of the corner of his eye. He stood up, taking his finger off the saw trigger, letting it spin down slowly until the only sound left in the room was a deafening silence.

"Merry Christmas," Russell said in a low voice. He seemed only mildly surprised to see her. Without a word, Rebecca continued to study the room. She picked up a couple of toys and then stepped to a bulletin board covered with yellowing newspaper clippings. She began to read the articles. One by one they chronicled the exploits of the mysterious stranger called Secret Santa. Rebecca just stood there, dumbstruck, as if she'd just learned English and wasn't quite ready to speak.

"There's a couple of yours up there," Russell acknowledged.

"The answer was right in front of me the whole time. I just couldn't see it," she said with disbelief.

Russell smiled. "I'm thankful for that."

"But, all these years . . . how did you afford . . . ?"

"On my salary?" Russell said, reading her mind. "The hard thing about working at a rest home is you find yourself taking care of people you know are never gonna walk out. To these people, I become family. And, when they die . . ."

"They leave you money," Rebecca finished his sentence.

Russell nodded. "Sometimes. The first time it happened was back in 1987. A man named McAbee passed away. About a week later, his lawyer called me up and said I had some money comin' to me." Rebecca nodded as Russell continued, "But I didn't feel right about taking that money."

Rebecca wrinkled her brow. "But it was yours . . . legally."

"Maybe so. But the way I see it, I didn't earn it . . . so, it wasn't really mine."

"So you found another use for it."

"Everybody needs a little helping hand now and then—so I invented Secret Santa. And all these years, I only told one living soul."

"One?"

"You see, I needed somebody to set up an account out of town so I could keep my secret . . . secret."

"Carter!" Rebecca said. "I knew he had a hand in all this."

Russell hung his head as if there was something weighing heavily on his mind. "I guess it wouldn't do me any good to ask you . . . not to publish your story."

Rebecca felt a knot tighten in her stomach. In the excitement of the discovery, she had almost forgotten— she had a job to do. She wanted to put his mind at ease, tell him not to worry, but she couldn't. "Russell, I'm a reporter. My assignment was to find Secret Santa. And I always complete my assignments."

Russell let her words sink in and then he managed a rueful smile. "Well, I guess . . . it was fun while it lasted."

Their eyes met for a moment, and Rebecca had the urge to pour her heart out to this gentle man, to unload all her fears and doubts and disappointments on his kind shoulders. Then the cab's horn rudely jolted her back to reality. "I should go," she said, her voice cracking. Russell nodded sadly, knowing the fate of Secret Santa was in her hands.

Rebecca walked quickly to the door. She was afraid that if she hesitated for another second she'd lose control, like the little girl who found out her beloved St. Nick was just an overweight phony with a tacky red suit and a fake beard. But at the doorway she stopped and turned back. There were still questions left unanswered. "Russell, why . . . why'd you do it? I mean, what's in it for you?"

Russell pondered the question. She could see his mind percolating as if he'd never really considered the matter before. "For me? Just about everything, I suppose. The way I look at it . . . giving is its own reward. And I've never found anything that makes me feel that good . . . inside. There's nothing else like it, really."

Rebecca felt humbled. "So tell me, what's at the top of Secret Santa's list this year?"

Russell studied the laces on his work shoes. "A waitress needs a job . . . and Hamden needs a diner. I couldn't think of anything better."

Rebecca's eyes lit up as the realization hit her. "So *you're* the one who bought Charlie's. *You* own the diner?"

Russell shook his head. *"Owned.* I deeded it over to Callie this morning."

Rebecca looked into his eyes and was overcome with the strange feeling that maybe Callie was right after all. She recalled the young waitress' very words: "It was an angel." Russell Washington was an angel on earth—a good-hearted, noble soul without a selfish bone in his aging body. A simple man, living a simple life in a small town just east of noplace in particular. Secret Santa had just come to life in the heart of a cynical reporter.

As she stood staring at him, Russell winked at her as if to relieve her of any journalistic culpability. Then he flipped his goggles back down over his eyes, and the saw roared to life once more. It was, after all, the morning of Christmas Eve and there was much work to be done before nightfall.

Just before she walked out the shed door, Rebecca whispered a final good-bye. "Merry Christmas . . . Santa."

CHAPTER 20

A Salvation Army Santa lethargically jingled his bell, working the last remnants of holiday shoppers on the sidewalk outside the *Indianapolis Sentinel*. Inside the newsroom, Rebecca sat at her cubicle with an Olde Hamden Inn postcard tacked to the wall and a Hamden snow globe serving as a paperweight. Her fingers were racing across her computer keys. Never had a story come so easily. Just as she stroked the last word and saved her file, the phone rang. "Rebecca Chandler," she answered. Her professional demeanor relaxed into a smile as she recognized the voice on the other end of the line.

"George? Hello. What a surprise. Merry Christmas to you too."

Bob was chewing on one of his wife's tofu Christmas cookies when Rebecca strolled into his office. "This is my last story," she said, plopping her copy on the desk in front of him. Bob looked up, waiting for her to smile, to tell him it was all some sick joke, to take it back. But he could tell by the look in her eyes—she was dead serious.

"I quit," she continued.

"What?" he said in his wounded voice. "You can't quit. You're my best feature writer."

"Oh, I'm sure you can find somebody else to cover your three-legged dog stories," Rebecca said, turning to leave.

"Wait," Bob said, desperation now creeping into his voice. Rebecca stopped and spun around to face him. "You've been hired away . . . haven't you?" he said accusatorily. "Let me guess: *The New York Times* . . ." Rebecca sighed and shook her head. *"The Wall Street Journal.* No. It's the *Philadelphia Inquirer,* I'm sure of it."

"The *Hamden Herald,"* Rebecca said confidently.

Bob glared at her like she was speaking Portuguese. "The what?"

"I'm the new editor. George Gibson's retiring and I'm taking the job."

"Are you crazy?" he said.

"Never been saner in my life," she assured him.

Rebecca gave her editor one last farewell smile. "Merry Christmas, Bob," she said, exiting his office.

Bob sat like a stumped game show contestant. "George who?" Then he picked up her copy from his desk.

Rebecca pulled her coat tight around her as she left the front door of the *Indianapolis Sentinel*. She noticed the Salvation Army Santa who now stood beardless, another victim of the Beard Bandit. That story, she thought, could be handled by her successor. She chuckled to herself and quickened her step, as if she suddenly knew exactly where she was going and was in a big hurry to get there. As she turned the corner, she thought of her Secret Santa story and wondered how it would play in Hamden.

The next morning, the good people of Hamden rushed to retrieve the *Indianapolis Sentinel* from their doorsteps. There, on the bottom half of the front page, was Rebecca's story. They read quickly through the opening paragraphs chronicling in detail Rebecca's visit to Hamden.

There was the story of Harley's tow truck and Scotty's wings. And how, this year, Secret Santa had saved the town's diner. But there was more. . . .

"So, I set out on this peculiar journey. My assignment: to find the mysterious giver of gifts—known as Secret Santa. And, like the Magi of old, his gifts are more than simple gestures of goodwill, they are tokens that come from the heart of a man who's naïve enough to believe that, maybe, just maybe, the worthiness of a man's life isn't measured by the size of his bank account, but by the size of his heart. The journey led to this humble hamlet called Hamden, Indiana. This man's story is well-known in Hamden. For, like an old-time traveling salesman, he comes to call once a year, not to peddle encyclopedias or vacuum cleaners but to bestow a gift on some deserving neighbor in need. He asks no recognition for his good deeds, no accolades or pats on the back. He does it all for a simple feeling, the feeling that comes from finding happiness in another's good fortune. He asks nothing in return, save one request, that the secret he has kept so faithfully remain just that—a secret. For it is in his anonymity that Secret Santa sends a message to us all: Giving in its purest form expects nothing in return."

At the Corapeake Cove Rest Home, Russell finished reading the story and wiped a tear from his eye. He quietly folded the newspaper and said a little prayer of thanksgiving. For like the Magi, Rebecca Chandler had wisely chosen a gift to honor the sacrifice of love and the power of peace—the true meaning of Christmas. Tucked away in a tiny shed, a light would still burn giving hope to hungry hearts. And Secret Santa would remain just that—a secret.